TILT

Other Books by Ian Gouge

Novels and Novellas

Tilt - Coverstory books, 2023
Once Significant Others - Coverstory books, 2023
On Parliament Hill - Coverstory books, 2021
A Pattern of Sorts - Coverstory books, 2020
The Opposite of Remembering - Coverstory books, 2020
At Maunston Quay - Coverstory books, 2019
An Infinity of Mirrors - Coverstory books, 2018 (2nd ed.)
The Big Frog Theory - Coverstory books, 2018 (2nd ed.)
Losing Moby Dick and Other Stories - Coverstory books, 2017

Short Stories

An Irregular Piece of Sky - Coverstory books, 2023
Degrees of Separation - Coverstory books, 2018
Secrets & Wisdom - Paperback, 2017

Poetry

Crash - Coverstory books, 2023
not the Sonnets - Coverstory books, 2023
Selected Poems: 1976-2022 - Coverstory books, 2022
The Homelessness of a Child - Coverstory books, 2021
The Myths of Native Trees - Coverstory books, 2020
First-time Visions of Earth from Space - Coverstory books, 2019
After the Rehearsals - Coverstory books, 2018
Punctuations from History - Coverstory books, 2018
Human Archaeology - Paperback, 2017
Collected Poems (1979-2016) - KDP, 2017

Non-Fiction

Shrapnel from a Writing Life - Coverstory books, 2022

Ian Gouge

TILT

First published in paperback format by
Coverstory books, 2023

ISBN 978-1-7393569-0-3 (Paperback)
ISBN 978-1-7393569-1-0 (eBook)

www.iangouge.com

www.coverstorybooks.com

"This service is now approaching London King's Cross."

For most passengers the announcement is unnecessary. There has been general fidgeting since Alexandra Palace, and almost full-scale mobility from Highbury onwards. When the Guard heralds the train's entrance into the tunnel just north of the terminus almost all of its passengers are already on their feet, bundles of human impatience standing by the doors, in aisles, checking wallets and purses for tickets. Those who have chosen to take a more relaxed approach to disembarkation and the inevitable platform stampede that will follow are still switching off laptops, re-packing bags, or texting 'arrival' messages on their phones.

"London King's Cross will be our final station stop."

At the very rear of the train in the last First Class carriage, four people have chosen to adopt an even more disinterested stance toward their arrival. Had they been connected, all sitting together in a single block of seats, two pairs separated by a table upon which the combined detritus from the journey rested, such collective lassitude would perhaps have been understandable. As it is, they are geographically dislocated from each other.

Sitting separately across the last three rows of seats, at some point between North London and their emergence from the tunnel into mid-morning light they have each looked up, considered the queue already formed in the aisle, and contemplated their own movement. Having done so, the three who sit in the final two rows could hardly mistake the moment when the fourth of their number breaks rank and decides to shift. Although they would not have heard the sigh he omitted prior to doing so, they could not fail to see his struggle as he levers himself up from his seat and stretches for the overhead rack where a bag and a pair of crutches await reclaim. The smartly-dressed woman in the row immediately behind him and the man sitting across the aisle from her respond instantly.

"Let me get those for you," she says, quickly at his side and reaching for the crutches. That her offer is a reversal of the traditional notion of men helping women is not lost on her - nor is the fact that, in these days of supposed equality, such gentlemanly gestures are sadly on the wane.

Her actions are complimented by the second man reaching for the accompanying bag which, when it emerges from its resting place, is revealed to be a smallish rucksack. It is surprisingly light.

"There you are," he says unnecessary as he places it on the table.

"Thanks." Shuffling further up the aisle just ahead of them, the bag's owner slips his arms through its straps and takes the crutches from the woman. "Much appreciated."

Watching him as he swings himself along the carriage to join the end of the queue, his two assistants exchange a brief smile before returning to corral their own belongings and then follow the semi-incapacitated man towards the front of the carriage.

And the fourth? He remains seated throughout, content to watch the little pantomime unfold before him, a slight smile playing upon his lips. If you were to judge by the look on his face you could have been forgiven for assuming that something in the interplay he just witnessed has mildly amused him; but that would be to misinterpret his expression.

There is something other than amusement which has struck him. Whether or not he is inclined to think anything further of it is a question relegated to oblivion when the train finally draws to a halt. Looking out through the window one last time, he offers his own sigh before easing himself from his chair and, with some resignation, prepares to submit himself to the remainder of his day.

"This is London King's Cross. All change please. All change."

~

10:00

Toby pauses on the platform to adjust his grip on the handles of his crutches. It is an action which has become automatic, one undertaken without thought or premeditation - and one he hopes will soon be relegated to history. Ahead of him a wave of his fellow travellers pulses toward the barriers, and in spite of the inevitable hold-up awaiting them, he is surprised how quickly they seem to move, the gap between him and them growing rapidly. The man and woman who helped him gather his things as they approached the station have already accelerated beyond him, soon to be absorbed in the throng. He thinks he remembers one other traveller in his carriage, but a quick glance over his shoulder reveals no-one. Perhaps he has already missed him.

With a sigh he drops into the swinging rhythm which has become second nature over the past few weeks, his initial stutterings and stumblings long since banished, trumped by a fluency which has impressed many - Dan, Huw and Matthew among them. Toby wonders if they have been more impressed by his mastery of this new and enforced mode of perambulation than his ability to get a little late in-swing on his medium-pacers. From time-to-time the latter has forced them to succumb to unrestrained approbation, most noticeably during that remarkable match against Old Cuthbertians when it seemed he could do no wrong. The bright red Dukes' ball had jagged back off a length three times in the space of two overs, each time to devastating effect.

But that had been some while ago, and since then he has begun to experiment with a greater degree of variation in his delivery in an increasingly desperate attempt to recapture that now legendary magic. Odd bouts of success have kept him motivated, though the match with Bourden Park 2nds had not been one of those. Forced into relying on an excess of effort in order to maintain a modicum of unplayability had, in the end, been his downfall.

Perhaps the weakness had been there for months, if not years; perhaps it had been lying in wait for him, just for that precise moment when he slammed his foot down at the end of his fourth and final over and his Achilles ruptured. Even now, swinging along platform four at King's Cross, he recalls the agony, his collapse, and the instantaneous laughter from both Dan and Matthew - until they realised he hadn't simply fallen over and was in serious trouble. Even now he tells himself had he known what was in store for him, he would have eased back a little, sacrificed pace for accuracy in the belief that he still has the ability to 'tie down one end'. That afternoon Bourden had been in the ascendant and looking as if they were going to chase down the required total with ease; thus, with his team facing defeat as a result of an earlier batting collapse, nothing but maximum effort was acceptable.

But he hadn't known what was coming, he couldn't see into the future - which on one level was ironic given that as an Actuary his whole reason for being was to do exactly that. Yet the skills required to be effective in his job were gradually being diluted, expertise replaced by invisible algorithms behind anonymous computer screens; rates, predictions and monthly pension figures were now arriving at the press of a button. Swinging towards the tail of the diminishing queue at the barrier, for a moment he tries to parallel his professional life with cricket in order to conjure a sporting metaphor that would fit the former perfectly.

Pausing at the automated gates, he takes both crutches in his left hand and retrieves his ticket from a trouser pocket. At first reluctant to be accepted, it is suddenly sucked into the machine and then almost instantly spat out from a different slot. The barriers crash back somewhat abruptly and he levers himself through in an awkward jumble of legs and metal poles, retrieving the ticket along he way. Liberated into the open spaces of the concourse, Toby takes a moment to recalibrate, returning the ticket to his pocket and a crutch to each arm. Although he knows his passage through the barrier would have appeared somewhat comical to most onlookers, he is encouraged to have passed the test without mishap - and certainly with much more fluency than the last time he tried it! More than that, it is an episode - however brief - which has reinforced his impatience for a future without reliance on artificial supports.

In many ways this ambition represents a return to the past rather than a foretelling of the future. As he heads across the concourse towards the taxi rank, he briefly imagines a situation where all the computers at work are suddenly discovered to be fallible and, as a consequence, his expertise is elevated in importance once again. And he sees himself pounding in from 'the playground end' once more, the swing he is able to conjure from the hard-seamed ball manifesting itself even later and with more devastating effect than before. Whether or not he is prepared to concede both are fantasy, they remain scenarios which give him something upon which to lean - as much as he leans on his crutches in order to facilitate him getting from A to B. Attaching himself to the end of a queue where everyone is focussed on the flow of black cabs parading before them, he wonders for a moment whether he might have become too reliant on his crutches and - God forbid! - too reliant on those computers; whether he might have inadvertently abdicated responsibility to them for both movement and doing his job. In the case of the former, he will find out soon enough.

"Royal National Orthopaedic Hospital," he tells the driver as soon as he is settled in the back of a burgundy cab, momentarily grateful for the over-large door through which he and his crutches have passed without incident.

"Bolsover Street?" the cabbie says unnecessary before turning his attention to the road and moving them out into the traffic. There is the blast of another car's horn as they pass the entrance to the St. Pancras hotel.

Toby plays with the word 'Bolsover'. He went there once when on a Midlands tour with the team. Thanks to the weather, he had being forced to take a day off and, eschewing the impromptu card school his teammates had established in the hotel, chose to explore the castle instead. When had that been? Three years ago? Although not the only memorable event of that day, it is evidence of something that his inability to recall in detail the three matches they managed to play across that long weekend is of less importance than trying to forget all that which he knows he must. Although he cannot bring to mind his precise bowling figures in those matches (something which typically annoys him) he does remember some of the wickets he took - especially the unplayable delivery that had removed one of their opponent's openers thanks to a sharp catch by Matthew behind the stumps. It was a defining moment of sorts, and one he likes to regard as an individual link in a chain of such sporting moments. As the cab rattles along Euston Road, he can only yearn for the next.

They turn into Bolsover Street what seems like only moments later, Toby having been absorbed by both memory and the watching of pedestrians as they busied themselves on the pavements. He had been struck by the incongruous nature of the Euston Road underpass - as if such a thing could possibly exist in London! - and the ever-advancing modernity and scale of the buildings. Simultaneously the newer ones seem both self-aware and self-assured, and when the Orthopaedic Hospital appears before him, Toby is struck by how modest it looks. Indeed, without its tell-tale signage one could be forgiven for mistaking it as a Travelodge or some other budget hotel. As he emerges from the back of the cab to stand on the pavement Toby knows such an assessment would be unkind as well as inaccurate. Sorting out his arms and crutches once again, his imagination propels him through to the welcoming reception and then up in the lift to the third floor where he will sit in a small open area and wait to be called into Dr. Tyrell's consulting room.

The taxi ride having been made with such efficiency, on sitting down Toby needs to check his watch to confirm exactly how much time has passed since he stepped off the train. Thirty minutes or so. He nods as if in answer to an unspoken question and reconciles himself to a fifteen-minute wait. If there is one thing he can say about Dr. Tyrell it is that he is punctual to a fault. This is not, Toby knows, necessarily an attribute unique to his consultant, but rather one of the spin-off benefits of attending as a private patient, his treatment funded by the rather generous healthcare package offered by his company - and one which, when he took the job some thirteen years earlier, he had assumed he would never need. Immediately after the accident he had been treated in Peterborough, but there had been something out of the ordinary in the nature of his Achilles tear which had required further assessment. Even though it was in London, the RNOH had been identified by his insurance company as the most appropriate service provider. His first visit - during which Dr. Tyrell had 'reevaluated' some of the work carried out in Peterborough - had been painful and the journey home especially difficult. The second, around a month ago, progressed in a more satisfactory manner - except for the debacle of him falling through the barriers at King's Cross and needing to be helped to his feet by station staff. At least this time he had managed to negotiate that particular obstacle adequately enough, the only assistance from which he'd benefited was during the gathering of his things on the train - though from his perspective this had been unnecessary.

Ignoring the only other patient in the same waiting area, Toby lifts a couple of magazines from the low table beside his chair. From the front cover of one, a Premier League footballer stares at the camera uncertainly while his wife, all manicured and made-up, attempts to mimic bygone days when she had been a top model; days before she had borne the two children who are also looking outwards, a somewhat bemused expression on their infant faces. Had he, Marita, Alex and Lucinda been similarly photographed, Toby wonders what sort of pose they might have adopted. The children would undoubtedly have been giddy and fidgety, each attempting to get the other to do something embarrassing in front of the camera. And Marita? Not having the sort of pedigree enjoyed by the 'Wag' now smiling back at him, Toby imagines her expression as being somewhat doubtful, almost distrusting. Perhaps there was something in her history which such public exposure might have surfaced or which she would have tried to keep hidden - if so, he cannot imagine what it could have been. He would have smiled, of course, happy to adopt the pose expected of a proud husband and father. Was he not, after all, a 'team player'? Did he not have years of domestic and competitive experience to prove as much, and plenty of anecdotes to support that claim? Indeed, it would have been easy for him to think of episodes with Dan, Huw or Matthew not only to confirm as much, but to bring a smile to his face. And an appropriate one at that.

His professional life was little different. On more than one occasion over the previous thirteen years he has, during his annual appraisals, been complimented on exactly that: how he put the team before himself; how he always considered the 'big picture'; how dependable he was. Even though such praise was one of Jack Welby's standard compliments, Toby believed there was more sincerity in it when applied to him.

"And don't think that outstanding effort of yours around the year-end has gone unnoticed, Wedgwood. I've put in a good word for you; you know, for a little above the standard increment. But then you also understand how these things are, don't you? Out of my hands at the end of the day…"

Honesty or smoke-and-mirrors? It depended how he was feeling at the time. But at least Jack was a relaxed enough boss to be happy to use his nickname even in formal situations. To most people at work he was 'Wedgwood' - and to everyone at the cricket club too.

He had told the story of the name's origins often enough for any frisson he'd once had in explaining it to have withered away. Not that the tale was anything remarkable. His surname - Kupp - came from mythological European roots many generations removed; his christian name - Tobias - was inherited from his grandfather. Combining the two together - 'T Kupp' - opened him up to all sorts of jokes which, when younger, he had chosen to interpret as ridicule. The journey to see them as evidence of friendship and acceptance had taken some time. Toby remembers a barrage of insults before he grew into his name: "a chip off the old tea-cup", perhaps a "crack-pot". As he was aspiring to be a particular kind of 'Toby', people were throwing other names at him, ones he consistently tried to bat away. In was 'Wedgwood' which had stuck early on however, the result of a school friend's family holiday to Shropshire which had included a visit to the Potteries. He had arrived back from his break with a dodgy accent and the ultimate nickname for his friend. Had the fact that 'Tobias' wasn't a million miles away from 'Josiah' made any difference? Toby isn't sure.

To the best of his knowledge Marita had always been Marita. She wasn't the kind of woman to embrace such laxity. Toby glances again at the precisely prepared woman on the cover of the magazine. Where she was curved, Marita was not; in her, well-defined angles dominated, to the extent that her face appeared hawkish and harsh, as if she were a witch hiding in plain sight. Which she wasn't, of course. Indeed, it was one of Toby's great regrets that others' first impressions of her were often more likely to be unkind than accurate. When he thinks of her as a wonderful mother - as he does now - it is not without a little guilt.

"Mr. Kupp?" Nurse Whitehurst appears silently from Tyrell's consulting room and offers a general smile. It is one which probably should be reserved for those uncertain moments when meeting people for the first time, yet she seems to have adopted it as her default. Even with the flicker of recognition aimed at Toby as he raises himself from his seat, it doesn't change.

Toby checks his watch - 10:45, bang on - then follows her into the next room.

"Tobias, how are we?" Tyrell stands and offers his hand. It is the consultant's standard opening, and Toby wonders if that is what all people do in defined circumstances - settle on easily repeated things to do, say, feel - as if such consistency relieves them of the need to be inventive. Or to think. Tangentially he recalls how the initial ball of his first over is always bang on middle stump, almost Yorker length, just to see what the batsman is made of. And then he wonders when he'll be doing that again.

"Pretty good," he offers, then waving the crutches adroitly, "considering."

Tyrell laughs.

"Well, let's see if we can't help you with those…" He indicates the examination table against the far wall and invites Toby to lay on it. Whitehurst relieves him of his crutches. "So the plan today is firstly to relieve you of that rather cumbersome ankle support you're wearing, then examine the Achilles, try some exercises to check your movement, and so forth." Tyrell pauses to examine some notes laid out on his desk. "Then, all being well - and it should be well after all this time - we'll provide you with a more comfortable, lighter support and a new set of exercises."

"And those things?" Toby, propped up on his elbows, indicates where the crutches are now resting in the corner of the room.

Tyrell, still smiling, chooses not to follow his gaze.

"You should leave here with just the one, I hope. After which - depending on how you get on with the exercises - you can wean yourself off that too."

"How long?"

"Until you don't need crutches at all? Perhaps a couple of weeks."

"No." Toby eases himself onto his back in accordance with an unspoken command from the nurse. "Until I'm fit enough to start playing cricket again."

At this Tyrell laughs.

"Immediately - if you want to be straight back here, that is." The doctor moves away from the desk and stands by the table, watching Whitehurst as she removes the velcro fixings and eases the thin cast from Toby's leg. "Look, the Achilles has to cope with phenomenal strain. Day in, day out, we take it for granted; we pound it and twist it and stretch it. Most of the time it doesn't complain. Sometimes it does. Just like yours did. Which means it's more likely to complain again in the future - and more readily too. So you need to take it easy." He pauses to signal approval to the nurse as she moves away from the table, then, conscious he hasn't answered Toby's question, looks directly at him. "Not before next season. Maybe some light training in the spring. But matches? July perhaps. Doctor's orders."

Reluctantly Toby nods, then, considering the ten months between now and then, finds himself looking up at the subtly Artexed ceiling. It was the answer he was expecting, but not the one he was looking for. He wanted to be ready for April. Could he stretch the definition of 'light training' perhaps?

"Maybe June," Tyrell softens. "But let's have a look first, shall we? Now, this may be a shade uncomfortable."

At first Tyrell's hands feel as if they are floating over his skin, Toby relaxing his foot in consequence and allowing the other man to manipulate it gently. However, when Tyrell first probes with his fingers just above the ankle, Toby cannot help but cry out.

"Sorry," Tyrell pauses, "but I did warn you." His fingers adopt a rhythm which briefly moderates the pain and turns it into pulses of mild discomfort. "I'm feeling the Achilles to get a sense of how well it has healed, to see if I can find any worrying bumps that shouldn't be there."

"And?"

Tyrell continues to push and prod for a short while longer before rising from his slightly crouched position.

"Pretty good," he says. "Not perfect, mind - these things rarely are - but as well as could be expected."

"Marks out of ten?"

The doctor laughs. Nurse Whitehurst, now at his side, smiles. Toby assumes it is another from her standard arsenal.

"I forgot you were a numbers man! That's the actuary in you speaking, I suppose."

"And the cricketer…"

"Ah." Tyrell bends again and starts manipulating Toby's foot with one hand whilst keeping the other pressed to the area around his heel. "An odd combination, don't you think? Actuary and cricket, I mean. Not the numbers part, of course: but I'd always considered one to be quiet, considered, calculating; the other more aggressive, explosive."

"I hadn't thought of it like that," Tony confesses, struck how such an intelligent and personal observation was unlikely to be ventured under the NHS. Perhaps that was one of things you paid for, the individual touch. And Nurse Whitehurst's glossy professionalism.

"Out of ten, then?" Tyrell returns to the question. "Eight - if I'm being generous." He glances at Toby, the disappointment all too evident in his face. "I would never give a ten obviously, not after the damage. So an eight is pretty decent; almost as good as it gets. It might end up being a seven - though that depends on you. If you don't keep up the exercises - and if you rush back to the crease too soon - it could be worse than that." When Toby chooses not to reply, Tyrell says "I've made myself clear?"

"Yes."

"Good." Tyrell smiles reassuringly and moves back toward his desk. "Now Becky will walk you through some exercises and so forth, then we'll pop an elasticated support on and you can be on your way. Anything planned for the rest of the day?"

~

Imogen wonders why the man with the crutches had seemed less than appreciative when receiving her help. Once he had sorted himself out he seemed to manage well enough, even if his descent from the train had been a little awkward. Maybe he was one of those fiercely independent people who simply *had* to manage on their own and so her intervention had been unwelcome. She could sympathise to a degree. Or then again, perhaps he had simply been distracted; or possibly he had been asleep and their arrival in London had come to him out of the blue. Whatever the reason, she knows distraction is something she cannot afford to countenance today; she has to be on her mettle, prepared for anything. And she believes she is. During the short journey down from Stevenage she had read and re-read her CV; she knows it so well that, if pressed, she suspects she might be able to recreate it from scratch, pretty much word-perfect. Those attributes - a good memory and attention to detail - are important for an Executive Assistant to possess. She has used the paper history of her professional life to rehearse responses to the questions they might ask her. Standard ones about 'greatest strength' or 'greatest weakness', her proudest achievement, what colleagues would say about her, or an example of when she had faced her greatest challenge will all be easy enough to handle; but it is those which might come at her from left-field that give her the most concern simply because she cannot imagine what they might be. How do you prepare for something you can't see coming?

Keen to catch-up on the throng ahead of her, as she walks toward the ticket barriers Imogen checks her watch. They had arrived on-time, which was good - but now she has two hours to kill before the interview. She might have taken a later train but had decided to leave nothing to chance. Engineering works having overrun the previous weekend, Network Rail had warned of potential delays coming into town. The train she had chosen had given her an hour's leeway in the event of a hold-up. Again, it was all about preparation. Unfazed at being so early, she pulls her ticket from her purse and joins the queue at the barrier. Having already devised a plan to cater for a punctual arrival, she finds herself relaxed, calm: she will take the tube to London Bridge then find a café in Borough Market for a coffee before heading to The Shard. It will be another opportunity to think things through and be ready.

Following the signs for the Northern Line, Imogen allows herself the luxury of reducing her pace a little, abstaining from a full-throttle walk in order to take in her surroundings and the people around her. Not being a regular visitor to London, the capital still possesses certain frisson, and she watches the crowd to see if she can divine those for whom the city is a new experience. For the majority it is clearly not. There are hoards walking head down, seemingly in a well-worn groove - which is where she might find herself soon enough, depending on how the interview goes. Filtering out men, tourists, and all those in jeans or t-shirts, she tries to focus on the other professional women she can see. There seem to be a preponderance of suits of one kind or another, and more trousers in evidence than she had expected. She is able to delineate the population further, largely through the cut of their clothes, the quality of their make-up, and their physique. As she waits on the southbound platform for the train that will take her to London Bridge, she tries to predict which women will get off at Bank - assuming the City is a magnet for them - and then imagine what their jobs might be. Imogen thinks it is easiest to spot those who work in sales or marketing: they will be slimmer, with heavier make-up, taller stilettos. Those in merely administrative roles will be at the other end of the spectrum, taking less care in how they look, unexceptional and run-of-the-mill. And the EAs and PAs like herself? Somewhere between the two: smart but not too showy, confident but not flashy. For a moment she wonders if it is the same in Stevenage. If the same templates apply there, undoubtedly they are taken up a notch in London owing to the increased competition. An image of Sonia pops into her head. There is something about her appearance which - in Stevenage at least - suggests she is managerial, experienced, professionally superior. Imogen suspects that in their provincial environment it is probably self-evident that Sonia sits a rung higher than her on the ladder. But in London? Based on appearance alone, where would Sonia sit? Settling on an answer, Imogen allows herself a smile; Sonia would be mid-division, at best.

But if that was the case, what did it imply as far as she is concerned? Once on the tube she takes the opportunity to examine her reflection in the carriage windows as the train enters the first tunnel. Clothes, make-up, physique - the three criteria on which she has settled. Which is the most significant? Imogen has always assumed the former, though whether this is because she is uncomfortable with her body shape is an interrogation to which she is unwilling to commit - not that she would deny she is carrying a pound or two more than she might wish. Diets and the gym have never been effective for her in terms of shedding rogue inches, and so she has settled on being 'careful' in terms of what she eats. If only she were slightly taller! Being stretched out by just an inch or two would surely make all the difference. Not that she is noticeably overweight - at least not by any measure she chooses to apply to herself. 'Shapely' is the adjective on which she most frequently settles, and she knows she is well-proportioned; not being afraid to don a bikini on holiday is surely all the proof she needs. Having reaffirmed her silhouette, she glances around the carriage again and finds nothing to disturb this equilibrium.

Although her suit - dark blue, jacket cut with a mid-length tuck and fashionably low lapels to reveal a crisp white crew-neck top - may only be from M&S, but it is the best she owns;

were she to wear it at work she is confident it would outshine anything in Sonia's wardrobe. Yet it is for 'special' - which means she has only worn it four times: one wedding, two non-London interviews, and today. How it compares to the clothes of those women now gathering by the doors in readiness for the train's arrival into Bank is another matter. Most of her tube-travelling contemporaries (she judges the majority to be in their late-twenties to mid-thirties) seem to have the sartorial edge on her: the cut of their clothes is slightly sharper, the colours more vibrant, the material from which they are made more refined. Imogen constructs a scenario where she will need a new wardrobe, and a little flutter of excitement runs through her.

And make-up, that third element? Given it is so flexible, impermanent, and open to change at the drop of a hat, surely it is the least important. Not one for going overboard, she prefers an understated approach to her foundation, blusher, mascara and lipstick, though today she has indulged in slightly darker eye-shadow and marginally redder lipstick. Attractive but not showy; appropriate rather than flirty. As the tube doors open at the station and the exchange of passengers takes place - like a trade of prisoners across a border - she smiles to herself; make-up? No issue. Indeed, she has no issue with the package as a whole nor the image she will present to those who will be interviewing her. Surely they will see a smart, professional-looking and not unattractive woman of thirty-three - which is exactly what she wants them to see.

Glancing up at the route map above the now closed doors, she registers London Bridge as the next stop. Automatically she checks her watch. In control - and feeling relaxed as a result - Imogen removes the filter with which she has been examining her fellow passengers for the last few minutes and casts her eyes about the carriage once again. A figure at the next set of doors brings her up short and she feels her heart quicken. Although it cannot possibly be Emma, the woman standing not that far from her - one hand on an open book, the other holding an upright for support - is the spitting image of one of her sisters. Undoubtedly this incarnation is a little younger, but in the shape of her features, the way she frowns as she reads, Imogen cannot fail to be reminded of her sibling. It is recognition which, for a moment, forces her back into the self-examination from which she has just emerged: if she and this other person were to be standing side-by-side, would people assume they were from the same stock? Recognising the connection between Louise and Emma had never been a problem; indeed, there was a period of time when - given they were born just a year apart - one could be forgiven for assuming they were twins. Theirs was a mould broken with Emma's birth, however; and when Imogen came along four years later, it was evident from relatively early on that she was going to be different. By the time she was in her teens her physical profile was well enough set for her mother's earlier assurance - "you *will* be like them, just give yourself time" and "you've still got a lot of growing to do" - to dissipate like smoke. Imogen was slightly smaller, slightly stockier, her eyes slightly closer together, her lips slightly thinner... She could go on but choses not to. The appearance of Emma's spectre is torture enough.

And why couldn't it be Emma standing there - in addition to fact that this version of her sister is at least eight years younger? Because Emma is now living in Zurich with her Swiss husband and their perfect children in their perfect home not far from the Toblerone-like Alps. Nor could it have been Louise who, as a result of her second marriage and a somewhat ruthless streak, now found herself on the faculty of a Californian University where she had risen to Vice-Principal and was rumoured to be heading for the top job in less than five years. Zurich, California, Stevenage. Even the words had a different quality about them.

Although at first in awe of them, Imogen grew-up despising her sisters. Not only was she the baby of the family, but she was less attractive, less athletic, and - most importantly from their perspective - less intelligent. She was cannon-fodder when they needed to pick on someone, when they wanted to demonstrate their superiority. Imogen provided the two of them with the chance to become even closer - comrades in arms, co-conspirators - all of which merely increased her own isolation. Louise taking a year out after A-levels allowed Emma to catch up on the academic timetable, and so the two of them started at the same university at the same time. During the three years which followed, Louise and Emma grew even closer, fed off each other, competed with each other - and as a result left Imogen even further behind; the Imogen who could never quite get the grades and who seemed destined to be rooted to Hertfordshire. Left behind in the geographic sense too. London might not have been Zurich or California, but at least it wasn't Hertfordshire. It was a city might just offer Imogen her last chance to move up. Or to escape. Waiting for the train to slow so that she can liberate herself, she returns her attention to her reflection in the window and wonders if getting away from home is the main reason why this interview is so important to her. It will mean escaping from Sophie, from Stevenage, and getting away from home too - a home with so many unhappy connections. It will also represent following in her siblings' footsteps, though in her own way. She has often wondered how things might have turned out had she been able to make it to university herself. Surely Louise and Emma would have been forced to see her in a different light rather than have their suspicions and theories - centred on her inferiority - confirmed. During holidays between college terms, tales were told of parties, adventures and romances, experiences from which Imogen would forever be excluded and for which she would have to substitute inferior alternatives. She glances down at her M&S suit. For the first year or so her sisters revelled in ensuring that she understood where she would be missing out, and therefore how increasingly superior they were to her. Whether correct or not, Imogen is sufficiently self-aware to understand that such chit-chat and tittle-tattle became truth for her and a burden has she carried around with her ever since. And now an interview in London; a real chance to slip the shackles.

As the train decelerates and the platform lights burst into the carriage, she checks to her left. Emma's doppelgänger remains motionless. Imogen sighs with relief. What if this other woman had also been getting off here? Perhaps Imogen might have travelled one stop further and then walked back, after all she had the time. But as it is she is released into London Bridge station, pauses on the platform to locate the 'Way Out' signs, then follows the crowd upwards to the ticket barriers after which she stops again, this time to consult a map. The Shard. Borough Market. In as close proximity as she had expected them to be. "That's good," she tells herself in an attempt to realign with her original plan. All that mattered now was that plan and its perfect execution.

Leaving the station with the pinnacle of The Shard behind her, Imogen heads along St. Thomas' Street, beyond the entrance to Guy's hospital, and towards Borough High Street. Rather than being a reflection of her fantasies about the well-heeled City, she wonders if this new scene is the authentic, working London. There is an edge to the bustle; the buildings seem coated with a semi-transparent layer of grime; taxis busy themselves diving through impossibly small gaps; even the smartly-dressed seem a little drab. Glancing over her shoulder, she can't help but contrast this picture with the gleaming precision of the modern edifice behind her. It is almost as if The Shard had been dropped into the middle of the city by an alien race simply to boast, to show how things could be, as if there were a lesson to be learned. She wonders what Victoria would make of it all; the Victoria she had known since she was a child and who had never been outside of Stevenage other than to go to Luton airport and fly off on a cheap package deal to the Costa del Somewhere. "London!" she had said when Imogen finally summoned up the courage to tell her friend about the interview; "I've always wanted to go to London". And then for a while she had sulked at the thought of Imogen leaving - which only fuelled the fire of Imogen knowing what was she was planning to do was totally the right thing. Victoria would hate the grime and not understand The Shard.

Waiting at the lights to cross Borough High Street, the apparently random collection of buildings facing her on the other side of the road disappoint her, though she is not exactly sure what she had expected. Perhaps given its proximity to her ultimate destination, she had assumed that 'Market' would be no more than a quaint term adopted by a gleaming new mall in a considerate nod to history. Yet once she is across the road and heading through a red-brick arch which opens out onto part of the market itself, Imogen finds herself encroaching on the past. Many of the original sheds remain; here and there some have been tarted-up in recognition of their twenty-first century clientele - yet in spite of the face-lift, they remain true to their origins. Walking around aimlessly for a few minutes, she is soon out onto Stoney Street unsure how to process her disappointment. Checking her watch and finding it to be just before eleven is sufficient to validate that she remains on schedule. Reassured, she recalls that the next step on her plan was to be coffee before a return to The Shard where she has been told to arrive at least fifteen minutes before her interview time in order to allow for the prerequisite security checks. Not having found an acceptable establishment in the heart of the market, she is back scanning the High Street before she settles on a café just to the left of the arch through which she had recently passed. It not being a chain, she is immediately charmed by its somewhat quirky nature, and is soon established by the window looking out onto the main road, a latte on the table in front of her.

~

Lawrence walks the platform in the wake of the woman in the blue suit who had also helped their fellow passenger with his crutches. Watching her as she puts distance between them, he sees her movement as more of a march than anything else, filled with purpose. From behind, he briefly hears the clicking of crutches, and characterises his own walk as somewhere between the two: neither determined nor encumbered. It is, he supposes, 'normal' - though if such a thing exists, it is actually a concept he finds difficult to make concrete. In the library he encounters all sorts, from the well-heeled and studious to those just killing time or wanting to get out of the rain. It is a refuge for many - and for the disadvantaged, more a place of sanctuary than one of learning. While it is entirely feasible to divide his customers into groups of one persuasion or another, it remains impossible to ascribe a common attribute to all of them. Perhaps they are equally 'normal' in their own unique way.

Which is certainly how he sees himself. In any in-depth analysis - not that he would submit himself to such a thing - he believes he could not be assigned any trait which might be regarded as renegade, dangerous, or imaginative. Even his familiar, 'Larry', is used by very few people, and it will be interesting to see how Tessa and Dylan choose to greet him in an hour or so. Watching the woman walk and finding himself comparing her gait with his own, Lawrence slips into musing about his other characteristics. If he were to describe himself how might he shape up? And how far from a mythological 'normal' would he stray?

Some thirty metres from the barrier he pulls his wallet from his trouser's back pocket and removes a ticket. It is precisely where he knew it would be, located in exactly the right space - after all, his is a wallet which is compartmentalised, well-organised. Which is one thing he would say about himself: he likes order - no surprise given his profession demands strict adherence to the alphabet and the Dewey classification system, both of which have dominated his life for the last eighteen years. Yet surely such a profile hardly compromises the borders of normality! As he waits for his turn at the barrier, Lawrence watches those - like the woman in the blue suit - who have already made it through; people of all shapes and sizes, and when it comes to what they are wearing, in various guises and disguises. He has a brief flashback to the somewhat flamboyant gentleman who had also been in his carriage, and who, on arrival, had been slower than any of them to move. Not that he has the imagination to fabricate one, Lawrence is sure there is much of a story hidden there as there will be in the throng before him now: an ageing hippy couple; three teenage girls competing to see who can show off the most midriff; the sharp and not-so-sharp suits, each punctuated by flashes of colour in shirts or ties or socks. He has never really been drawn to colour in that way. For him colour represents the antithesis of substance, and substance is what's important. Does such a philosophy make him more or less normal? He doesn't really know. As he slides his ticket into the machine, he cannot help but catch a glimpse of the sleeve of his herringbone jacket, the cuff of his pale blue shirt, the darker blue of his chinos. "There you are then," he says to himself as if such evidence is incontrovertible proof of something conclusive.

As soon as he enters the bowels of the underground, Lawrence seeks out a tube map to plot his route. Lincoln is far enough away from the capital for him to be a rare visitor, so he is not one of those frequent travellers confident enough to saunter into the tube and then ad-lib his way from A to B. They are meeting at 'Giraffe' - according to Dylan a restaurant near the London Eye - and he has been told he should head for Waterloo and follow the signs for the National Theatre. London being very much home turf for both Dylan and Tessa, Lawrence was already on the backfoot when he plucked-up the courage to ask them to meet him; as such, he could hardly object to their choice of venue, after all, they were unlikely to come to Lincoln. Finding Waterloo on the map, he settles on the notion of staying with one colour and one line, so picks the Northern: one stop north to Euston, then southbound to Waterloo. Although he has included Zone 1 travel on his return ticket, he is still slightly apprehensive when he presents it to the barrier which stands between him and the tube trains. Imagining it being eaten by the machine, he sees the outcome as having to engage in a difficult and embarrassing conversation with a member of staff in order to try and retrieve it. In consequence, when the ticket slides into and out of the machine without issue, he cannot but help register relief before seeking out the 'Northern northbound' signs.

Having to wait five minutes for the train, by the time it arrives the platform is a mass of impatience. As the doors slide open, where he had hoped to find space Lawrence can see nothing but bodies - and then suddenly there is a flood of humanity, dozens of people disembarking, dozens more taking their place. Standing pressed against an end partition, he looks along the carriage length to find an echo from the concourse above; not exactly the same hippy couple or trio of girls, but others who could take their place easily enough, as if travelling in London was a continuous cycle, each person a stand-in for another. He looks to see if there is anyone on the train who might pass as his doppelgänger: conservatively dressed, of average dimensions, feeling slightly out of place. Or normal. Depending on your perspective. There are a few candidates, and Lawrence wonders what they might think were they to look his way. Might they also see him as a mere duplicate of someone else? Even themselves? But then there are those who cannot be replaced. Ever. And as the train moves off he wants to think of his mother and of why he has come to London, but the noise of the train and the proximity of its passengers prevent any reflective thought.

At Euston the pantomime of the tube's disgorging old and then swallowing new is repeated, though this time he is one of those alighting. He takes the short walk to the southbound platform and gets there just as a train arrives. Although busy, it is marginally less crowded than the one from King's Cross, something which permits Lawrence to relax just a little more. He checks his watch. If he goes directly to Waterloo he fears he will be at the restaurant early, and even though they will only be having coffee, he has no desire to get their first. Checking the schematic above the seats opposite, he remembers Dylan had mentioned the option of alighting at Embankment and walking to the south side of the river via the Charing Cross railway bridge: "in case you want to stretch your legs after the train". It is a notion which - although dismissed at the time - now strikes him as being a good one. Warren Street, Goodge Street, Tottenham Court Road, Leicester Square, Charing Cross, Embankment. Surely he will be ready to get off at that point?

When he eventually emerges from Embankment station into daylight and feels the breeze coming off the Thames, he can do nothing other than omit a sigh of relief. Pausing to locate the steps up to the bridge, he takes in the view across the water: the London Eye, the concrete monstrosities of the South Bank complex, Waterloo Bridge, and then, away to his left, hints of other landmarks - the Oxo tower, Tate Modern, the sharp finger of The Shard. It is a skyline which has changed over the years, certainly since they first came here as a family, the five of them. He had been perhaps six or seven. Pausing part-way across the bridge as most visitors do, he tries to recall what it might have looked like back then, certain that his parents would have done their best to point out the landmarks. Unlike Dylan and Tessa who, via their different routes, eventually settled in London full-time and now call it their home, he has returned no more than six or seven times. Had he stood on this very spot on each visit he might be able to conjure an almost certainly inadequate time-lapse composition of the view, but all he is able to do now is make assumptions as to what is new and what is old. The resulting inaccuracy is annoying. Since that initial childhood visit he had been to London with his parents just once more; it had been a compensatory trip. Dylan had just finished his first year at university and taken himself off to America with some friends, and Tessa had been on an exchange visit in the Dordogne. It was his mother's suggestion that they make the most of the opportunity and take him to 'see the museums'. Even though his father had not been keen, that was what they had done. It proved a long and tiring day dominated by trains and crowds. He recalls the buttons of the Science Museum and the skeletons of dinosaurs, but not the river. The day after the visit as the three of them recuperated at home, he remembers thinking that for once his father had probably been justified in his reluctance. Not that he is in any position to confess as much to him now, given he doesn't know where he is. Neither can he consult his mother, who has been dead for over two years. Which was when everything changed.

Down-river a barge struggles against the running tide and, transfixed, Lawrence is mesmerised by the wake it creates. There is something irresistible in its movement, its navigation, just as there had been about his mother. For years she had been his barge; he, her cargo. Rather than it being his father, she was the one who had steered their collective course, striving to achieve the best for each of them in turn. He wonders how much getting Dylan and Tessa through school and onto university had taken out of her. And how much their father had bled her dry over the years, a constant drip like a leaking tap. Although his own future had been similarly secured (via a degree in librarianship at Aberystwyth) perhaps there had been a hint of her shrinking even then, an inkling of what was to come some fourteen years later. He likes to tell himself he had foreseen her decline, which was why he had chosen not to move too far when he left home in 2004. But when he does so he finds himself confronted by an accusation of inactivity and impotence; that even as she gradually crumbled under the dual threats of his father's unreliability and the disease which was to eventually get the better of her, he did nothing to alleviate any pressure she might have been feeling. If there should have been a role reversal at any point - he the barge, she the cargo - then he failed both to see its need and thus act on it.

He glances down at the bridge supports below him, the river buffeting the stonework and being forced to find a way around. Another metaphor for his life with her? Or perhaps such an image suggests the more etherial and nebulous. If so, it is in consequence something upon which he struggles to settle. When she had become really ill in the winter of 2017 not only had his barge lost its captain, but God had jumped ship too. In the space of two years Lawrence lost both the anchors which had given him stability for some time; decades in his mother's case. His father - who had long since abandoned them when it became evident his mother's time was irreparably limited - hardly counted given he baled out as soon the opportunity arose. But God? That was a different story altogether.

Straightening, he resumes his walk across the bridge. Dylan and Tessa have never been interested in his relationship with God, not that Lawrence has shared it with them. At times he had felt as if he'd found an imaginary friend - but you kept quiet about imaginary friends in case you were thought to be slightly unhinged. Had he been? Is that how he had found God in the first place - or even the reason why God had abandoned him? During those last months before she died, he'd been swept along not by the fact of her illness nor his father's earlier absconding, but rather by his own denial of it. Although personally devastating, God also having quit the field would be of little consequence to siblings absorbed by the practicalities of their mother's malaise. He tries to recall a time when he had explained to them exactly what it felt like to be him at that moment; he tries but fails. At some point it became too late anyway; not only was he no longer talking, but Dylan and Tessa had stopped listening.

Their perspective on those last two years was entirely different of course. As his mother had deteriorated, they had stepped into the breach, taking turns to be on-hand, to offer her tangible links to both present and past. It was supposed to be a three-handed arrangement but - not entirely unlike his father - Lawrence gradually found himself withdrawing too. In his own mind however, his disappearance was retreat rather than abandonment, self-preservation rather than self-serving. He never ceased to love his mother, but found it impossible to accept that soon she would not be there; part of him wanted to magic the reality of her illness away. The illogical conclusion? If he refused to acknowledge it, to witness and indulge it, to pander to it, then how could it be a real thing? Perhaps it was a line he might not have taken if God had still been at his side.

As he closes in on the south side of the river, Lawrence pauses again; he tries to locate the barge he had seen earlier, but fails to do so. Beneath him the water rushes against the bridge just as it had a few minutes before. The clatter of a train heading out from Charing Cross assaults him as if for the first time, and he turns to the south to watch it move away, shepherding its passengers from the heart of the city. The London Eye, there in his peripheral vision, attracts his attention, its slow methodical movement in contrast to that of the train; perhaps such silent and undramatic motion was appropriate given the people in the pods weren't actually going anywhere at all. He can make out a queue at the base of the wheel, sees figures moving this way and that, each pursuing their individual agenda. Thinking Dylan or Tessa might be among them, he attempts to filter the crowd. A pointless exercise. He checks his watch. They might already be at the café. He wonders whether they would have arranged to arrive together, compared notes along the way. Perhaps they will have a plan of attack. Knowing he has none of his own, he suddenly fears he should have thought things through more thoroughly than he has. As if recognition of his ill-preparedness is a trigger, his legs take over and he finishes walking the remainder of the bridge.

~

"Tilt, Old Boy, 'once more unto the breech'." Yes, it's a somewhat hackneyed aphorism, but if you can't have a bit of fun with yourself who can you have fun with? Most people maintain internal monologues all the time, though few of them realise it - or have the imagination to see them for what they are. Unlike me. Take those last three from the train, each still visible as I stand here on the platform and gather myself for the coming foray; if they were trees and you were able to insert a tap into their bark and syphon off those thoughts and unspoken words, what stories would they tell? Or not, perhaps. After all, is it too much to assert that not everyone has enjoyed as colourful a life as I?

But back to their probable lack of imagination. Isn't that where I come in? If that rather prissy-looking woman in the high-street suit isn't capable of understanding herself - nor the grumpy guy with the crutches who seems all frustration - if they don't have the wherewithal to stand outside themselves and paint the picture of their lives, then I certainly do. Proven. Time and again. "Tilt, you cad, is that a smug smile I feel breaking out across that face of yours?" But even if it is, time to walk on, time to walk on. Nod of thanks to the guard. Does he recognise me I wonder? Unlikely. Though - if I may say so - you, Tilt, are blessed with something of a striking visage, filled to the brim with wisdom and experience. That's the portrait your elegantly-lined mug paints. Not to mention just a trace of Hollywood in your swept-back, lovingly cultivated slightly too-long hair, greying now à la Anthony Quinn. Not that I was ever in Hollywood - "still a dream, still a dream!" - nor an actor, not like dear old Mama who couldn't really help herself. Though clearly she passed on some of her genes; a touch of the theatrical never did anyone any harm, surely?

And how do we feel about this mass of humanity in front of us, queueing at the barriers in order to be released to go about their meagre little businesses? Yes, as I too will soon be. I know, Tilt, Old Boy, I know. But there are parallels and parallels, don't you think? Fishing for my ticket from the outer pocket of my jacket I am reassured by the feeling of the soft silk-like lining on my fingers, imagine the abundance of that same rose colour carried throughout the inner itself. Is it such a despicable thing to be satisfied by the merest glimpse of the jacket's subtle tweed in my peripheral vision? As I said, parallels and parallels.

It's funny how, no matter how often I'm in London, that first wall of sound, its sheer volume, takes me by surprise. Strange how its contrast with the station makes the latter seem so calm, at least on reflection. Even with those great hulking machines there's a certain peace about the platforms. I've always found that's a juxtaposition which works rather well, sound and silence. Especially when you spring it on an unsuspecting audience. More than once I've stood at the back of the stalls not to watch the play but rather to observe the people watching the play; then, when they jump, I can't help but think "you did that, Old Fruit, made them jump." It's like having a special power of some kind. I daresay there are other powers that might be more - what? - beneficial, but I'll settle for the one I've got. The one associated with me, and with my name. Even if it's not my real name, born out of a mistake - though not a mistake made by me, I hasten to add. When was the last time the Great Tilt made a mistake? Noah would have been a lad!

Once through the barriers and heading to Euston Road, I pause, look around for nothing in particular, and in doing so catch sight of the guy with the crutches heading towards the taxi rank. Rather him than me. Checking my back pocket for my wallet (a somewhat automatic reflex I fear) I begin to head west. The British Library is not far enough to warrant a cab, thought it could be a different story if it were raining. I wonder if that's why I checked my pocket; a wallet guarantees the ability to pay for a taxi - and to cover the cost of coffee if that tight arse Duncan doesn't cough for it. Even after all this time I've no idea why he likes the BL café for his meetings; presumably he thinks they confer a degree of cachet or respectability on his sordid little profession. Ask me if he's worth the twelve percent he charges and you know my answer! "Hello Tilt," he'll say, full of his habitual but shallow bonhomie, and then we'll be off with our usual few minutes of merry-go-round before we get down to business.

Once, in the very early days, he asked me about my name, said it couldn't be real. I told him it was as real as we wanted it to be. Or as I wanted it to be. He wanted to know its origins but I played hard to get - at least until he told me he couldn't make a payment into a bank account whose holder's name was not the name he chose to go by. Which was, of course, enough. Not that I consider it a nom de plume, not any more. Tilt is what I've called myself, what people call me, how I am *known*. That's more than a nom de plume in my book. So swearing him to secrecy - and on pain of losing my rather lucrative patronage - I told him about the mishap which in many ways had created both the name *and* me. I'm not sure I'd been that precious about it at the time, but as things moved on, transpired as it were, there seemed a greater distance between who I had once been and the person I'd become. "Tilt, Old Boy," I said to myself one day, "you've become a name!" So few people are aware of its source; after all, why do they need to know? What difference does it make to them? I wouldn't describe it as a secret per se, but… Ask me who I'd share it with and I'd be struggling to come up with any ideas. Certainly not any of these people charging head down on this bustling pavement, nor that person sitting against the wall wrapped in a blanket and with an empty McDonald's cup in front of them. Refugee or Unfortunate? Abused or Addicted? How do you tell these days? I confess I've stolen one or two such types in the past; you know, minor characters to add colour to some scene or other. A little bit like Shakespeare's comic characters; for light interludes. Not that I'm comparing myself… "Tilt, you Old Rogue!"

You take your life in your hands crossing the entrance to the St Pancras hotel. That black cab heading this way; bet he turns without signalling. There! "Don't toot me, mate!"

Slipping into the vernacular can be satisfying sometimes. I could have made my way through St Pancras itself of course, station-to-station as it were, avoiding Euston Road altogether. But then I would have missed my glimpse of the Shaw Theatre - visible just there, after crossing the Midland Road - which always gives me further opportunity to reminisce. Or bask. And what is life for if you can't re-live it occasionally? My first London show, transferred from home. I can see it now, my name in large letters on the outside of the building and shouting into the city: *"The Discomforted by Tilt"*. I daresay that drew a few people in, the originality of it. Pausing to turn into the courtyard of the BL, I strain to see what's on there at the moment. Something about African drummers, I think. Well, I don't suppose they expect a hit every day of the week. The name caused as much of a kerfuffle as the play; more, probably. Critics thought it a joke, a gimmick; they too wanted to know where it had come from. For a while it was like a lure on a line. There would have been little credibility in confessing it had arisen as a result of a printing error.

There are people all over the courtyard, sitting on benches, on the gently graduated steps. They hover around the pop-up coffee tent, the type which seems to proliferate everywhere these days and, once established, never go away. Hardly pop-up any longer. And though it's not exactly Capri weather, that doesn't seem to stop young ladies dressing as scantily as if it were - or perhaps they might be equally at home adorning the banks of the Tyne on a Saturday night. Ah, those were the days! The stories the Old Rogue could tell! *The Discomforted* was merely the start; a start born from Mama's too early death and her old Am Dram company's willingness to put on my first little play solely as a tribute to her. Or at least that's what they said - but the thing made it to London, didn't it? They had been preparing the PR material - posters, flyers, tickets - when, in a typically Am Dram way, some idiot lost control of his fingers over the keyboard and missed two letters out from my surname. Somehow they only realised their mistake after they'd printed enough material to make a re-print commercially prohibitive. Did I mind, they asked; after all it was only for a three night run in a little provincial theatre. Nothing was going to come of an arrangement to briefly honour - and then forever forget - one of their own. But then on the back of an unexpected triumph - and to their gawping surprise - enter stage left, the one and only Tilt! A legend was born! They subsequently made the most of their role in my debut.

Down the steps and into the somewhat hideous building where I submit myself to the scrutiny of those manning the desks, their uniforms endowing them with the authority to search whatever the hell they damn well want. For an instant I wonder what might happen if one refused to comply. But as I have nothing to declare (other than - what was it Wilde said…?!) I breeze through and into the main atrium. Interesting how noisy it is. Given this is ostensibly a library (and in the bowels it is, of course) wouldn't you expect calm, serenity? Instead there are too many pockets of conversation, a constant thrum fed by queues at the information desk and streams of bodies heading into and out of the shop. There's always a shop these days. People seem to need souvenirs. I wonder if Duncan's ever thought of souvenir china with my own mug emblazoned on it; or perhaps simply the word TILT in some funky bold font. Tomorrow's collectors' items today! Thinking of Duncan I check my watch. Nearly ten-forty. Given he's rarely on time there's no point in me going to the café tucked away a little beyond the foyer. I think the BL would prefer to regard it as a restaurant so might get a bit uppity if you declaimed "I'm going to the café" too loudly. Deciding to give him time, I veer to the left, steeling myself for a close encounter with the hoi polloi and the tat they seem to love so much.

In my opinion the spaces between things in the shop - displays, tables, shelves - are universally too small, resulting in an on-going chorus of "excuse me" mainly, but not exclusively, in English. Claustrophobic or not, I can't help myself but take some time to scan the merchandise with distain. Once you get beyond the bookshelves where the BL pays homage to 'The Greats', things go downhill. Not only are there the aforementioned mugs - with others' names on - but jigsaws, drawing books, cheap plastic toys designed to keep Little Johnny quiet for the thirty seconds before they break. There are small displays of jewellery of various sorts, and over by the window, scarves and tea towels; dry your porcelain with George Bernard Shaw! In certain combinations I suspect the tea towels and the tasks for which they are designed might go together quite well. What would be the best use for Virginia Woolf's face? As I pause by a display of what is somewhat disingenuously labelled 'original artwork' - a range of small animal sculptures crafted from what appears to be wire unevenly coated with some kind of resin - I am barged in the back by a large European woman who is unsurprisingly struggling to get by. She apologises under her breath in a language I can't quite recognise. There is clearly frustration in her voice. If not desperation. Perhaps she's a tourist who's had enough of the commercial side of London. It's only her tone which persuades me not to get cross, and I suddenly think of the National Portrait Gallery, the famous images of Joyce and Wilde, the acres of space in which they are presented. And the quiet. From there, it's a small enough leap to decide that I'll pay the NPG a visit once I've finished with Duncan; indulge once again in that little game where I try and decide where I'd like my own portrait to be hung should I have it painted one day. The leap also encourages me to abandon the shop, to move things along, my purposeful if not rapid exit drawing some attention. Not that they can possibly think I'm some kind of up-market shoplifter. I mean! They've only got to look at me. Would a shoplifter own a jacket of this style and quality?

As I get to within range of the café I see Duncan waiting by the entrance presumably for a member of staff to take him to the table he has reserved. I moderate my pace. What should one make of him, I ask myself; I mean, first impressions and all that? Largely unremarkable. Light grey suit, no pattern; pink shirt - very pale - no tie; brown shoes, edging too close to tan, especially with that suit. One could be forgiven for imagining he was in his early forties, though closer inspection would give the game away. He looks…competent. Whatever it is he does (and his attire offers no clues), the disinterested observer might easily get the impression of exactly that: competence. And, to be fair, he is. Certainly in comparison with that bastard Morgan Stubbs who I was so right to drop immediately after *The Discomforted* was a success: he thought *both* sides of win-win were supposed to be rewards for him. Duncan is fair, I'll say that much. And usually relaxed - though at this precise moment as he looks into the café, presumably scanning tables to try and locate me, he gives the appearance of being a little on edge. Deciding to do the decent thing, I move toward him in order to short-circuit his search. Then three things happen almost all at once: a waitress appears; I get close enough to utter his name; and

Duncan's hand goes up to acknowledge someone already
sitting at one of the tables.

49

11:00

Toby hadn't thought about plans for the rest of the day. The only thing he had been focussed on was making it to his hospital appointment; what came after would be entirely dependant on how the consultation went. With Tyrell's question helping him realise how nervous he'd been as far as the outcome of the visit was concerned, eight-out-of-ten suddenly seems like a result. Sitting on the edge of the bed half-listening to Whitehurst's chatter as he moves his foot in accordance with her instructions, he calculates his remaining time in London. Checking his watch to confirm it is now a little before eleven-fifteen, he has just under four hours before his return train leaves King's Cross. For a moment he thinks of getting an earlier one but instantly realises he is in no mood to face the hassle of doing so. Lunch, then. And given the nurse is insisting on him keeping active, Toby settles on a short one-crutch walk.

A few minutes later as he waits for the lift to take him back down to reception, Tyrell's observation as to the contrary natures of the actuarial profession and cricket comes back to him. Dismissing the fascination both hold for him in terms of the preeminence of numbers - even if one set is recording the past and the other predicting the future - he wonders how he is able to flit effortlessly between both worlds. In many ways they are, as the doctor suggested, diametrically opposed and call on different sides of his personality: at work, Toby sees himself as quiet, studious, a picture of concentration; on the cricket pitch he is busy, noisy, prone to overheat, always on the verge of action in being suddenly required to sprint or catch. Nevertheless, he tells himself there is something resembling calculation when he bowls, and that each of his deliveries is more than largely random output from mere muscle-memory. Even so, he has to concede that on one level the major strands in his life represent two sides of a single coin - though he is obviously not a Jekyll and Hyde character, irrespective of what happened that day in Bolsover. Were he a single personality man, what would his work/play combination look like: being an actuary and playing bowls perhaps, or playing cricket and earning his living as a trader in the city? In the time it takes for the lift to reach the ground floor he has already begun to isolate traits which may or may not be relevant in both cases: attitude to risk is there, as is responsibility, being calculating, wanting to win. And being a 'team player', of course.

Once through the Hospital's exit and out onto the pavement, the inevitability of London hits him again. It is not just the noise, the traffic, and the volume people which strike him so forcibly, but the sense of urgency and self-absorption inherent in them. And perhaps - in those three men standing across the road from him, or the vagrant shuffling south in the general direction of Oxford Street - there is a little menace too. As he shifts his weight he is reminded how he now has only one crutch and glances to his free hand almost with an air of accusation as if - either through carelessness or by failing to prevent a theft - it has betrayed him and lost what had become a critical support. Looking after the tramp shuffling away from him, Toby turns in the opposite direction and heads north towards Great Portland Street station; he will cross Euston Road there and head into Regent's Park. Not that the park will detach him from the essence of London, but at least he will gain access to a green and largely traffic-free environment, an ideal setting for him in which to become acquainted with his semi-liberation.

His first few steps are a little unbalanced, lacking rhythm, and he is slightly surprised when he recognises how much he has come to rely on using both his arms to walk. This is a fantastic notion of course. For a few steps he is forced to concentrate on how he moves his two feet and single crutch in concert, reacquainting his good leg with its independence while striving to find a satisfactory new pattern of movement overall. Thanks to his lighter ankle support, he also misses the additional weight he has been carrying around, and although he can still feel traces of Tyrell's manipulative fingers, the sense of increased freedom is palpable.

Crossing Euston Road in front of Holy Trinity Marylebone, Toby enters the park on the corner of Park Square East, then heads diagonally towards the Outer Circle. By the time he has crossed into the park proper he has begun to feel accustomed to life with just a single crutch, falling into a revised gait, one which allows him to put a little extra stress on his fragile tendon. From just ahead he hears the shouts of children, and then, a few yards later, the modest expanse of a playground opens out to his right. It is not especially busy, yet there seems to be something in the voices of the young which manages to cut through background noise. Generally it is the sound of fun and enjoyment, punctuated by the odd cry which seems to verge toward either anger or tears. Slightly distanced parents watch on with an air of semi-concern, falling into quiet conversation, connections made in a far more reserved way than those between their offspring. Toby pauses for a moment to absorb the fearless bravado of the young.

As he moves on, from off to his left and masked by a copse of trees, Toby hears the odd shout coming from the sports club's tennis courts and is further propelled back into his childhood. He discovered his love of games when a little older than the children he has just passed. It had crept up on him stealthily, worming its way into his psyche thanks to watching 'Match of the Day', highlights of England test matches, Wimbledon. Almost by accident he found he wasn't slow when it came to running, and his football and cricket skills proved to be not so shabby. The Eighties turning into the Nineties found him in the squads for various school sports teams, and as he walks away from the playground he tries to recall the first time he was selected as a substitute for the under-14s in both football and cricket. His father had never liked cricket much and admitted to having been a fair weather Arsenal fan since his own schooldays. Although Toby had never correlated his decision to focus on cricket as being in opposition to his father's preference for football, as he heads further into the park - accompanied by the rhythm of his footfall and the tap of the crutch on the path - he wonders whether his choice had been manifestation of some form of juvenile rebellion. Whether the case or not, what was indisputable was that during the last four years of senior school his appearances in first team matches proved to be limited, in spite of his squad status. He has told himself that as a result of conscious prioritisation he allowed sport to take a back seat during those final two years of upper-school study, and when he arrived at University, picking up cricket or football again as a serious endeavour never really crossed his mind. He made do with the odd semi-friendly game of squash and tennis to satisfy the competitor in him. Tyrell's observation echoes once more. Perhaps he had always been 'aggressive' - but in a good way. He liked to win, got a kick out of being on top.

Yet there is something else about those sporting school years which now bothers him. It is a question that has been haunting him recently, as if it has chosen to elbow its way into the void created by a period devoid of cricket. *Why* had he only made a handful of first team appearances? In the final analysis, was he no better than an average player, no matter how he judged his own talents? Under such circumstances surely ambition became an irrelevance. As he heads towards Chester Road and the Inner Circle, he recalls the game against Old Cuthbertians. Had his success in that match been a reflection of his true ability or merely a fluke? He wants to side with the former, his argument being that he has become a smarter technical operator since he was a youth, age having gradually eroded his pace. Yet Toby realises such a position is more cul-de-sac than answer; if true, what does it imply about how potent he will be in another year's time, post-injury? Surely a tad slower still. It is not an enticing prospect. He has played with his fair share of 'old timers', cricketers become just a shadow of their former selves. There is little sadder (he chooses not to say 'pathetic') than watching a one-useful cricketer find they are no longer able to bat or bowl, then unable to catch or run. Will that be him one day? Toby likes to think he will know the right time to hang-up his spikes; and of course when he does he will still be involved with the club, he is one of its lynchpins after all. And if he wasn't? If he didn't possess the influence he does, would he have been playing regularly there or - as at school - just be a member of the squad? There are one or two juniors showing considerable promise and who could soon supplant him. Another unrewarding train of thought, and one which arrives just as he emerges onto Chester Road, a minor unevenness in the path simultaneously causing him to stumble slightly.

Toby looks down to his crutch accusingly, wondering if he had lost his new-found rhythm over the previous few strides. Stopping, he tries to assess how he is feeling physically, hoping that doing so will provide him with a kind of reset - both of his stride and his current thought pattern. There is a dull sensation in his Achilles; it is not pain exactly - he is well aware what that feels like! - but rather something more positive. It is, he tells himself, what healing feels like. Using that notion to try and buoy his mood - and realising he is hungry - he turns towards the Inner Circle confident he will come across a café soon enough. Setting off with renewed purpose, he finds his stride, attempting to gauge the sensation in his lower leg as he walks on, striving to go a little faster as if doing so will accelerate the delivery of his eventual reward. When he arrives at a signpost indicating the route to Queen Mary's Gardens, Toby is sufficiently up-beat to follow it. What had he planned for the rest of the day, Tyrell had asked; well, at least he will be able to create some kind of positive narrative for Marita when he gets home.

Such intention is all very well, however the notion of his being no better than average at his beloved sport - and destined henceforth only to decline - assaults him again almost as soon as he is in the garden. He wonders what he can do about it. Considering himself good at problem-solving, he knows there must be a strategy of some kind to rescue him. Yet even that thought merely adds layers of difficulty. What if he is mistaken there too? What if his ability to work his way out of a tight corner or find the solution to an actuarial conundrum was also no better than average? Arguably circumstantial, he has evidence ranged against him when it comes to a reduction in cricketing prowess, but professionally? As he tries to concentrate on the herbaceous borders by which he walks, heading for the small lake he can see ahead, he cannot help but scan his recent professional past for clues. Hadn't Welby praised his efforts last Christmas? Wasn't he regarded as a 'team player'? Evidence for the defence then. But his pay rise hadn't exceeded the norm after all he'd said, so nothing exceptional there. And when he had floated the idea of going for a promotion within twelve months or so, Welby had been evasive. More than that, he hasn't been included on the task force recently set-up to review a potential new software package, one aimed specifically to support his exact area of expertise. Grist to the prosecution's mill. If the jury was indeed out, suddenly Toby didn't want them to come back in and deliver a verdict.

But this was crazy thinking! He stops at the edge of the lake and, leaning a little heavily on his crutch, tries to appreciate the view. Marita would like it here he tells himself. They hadn't been to London for years, not since they came when the kids were young. They had assumed the Natural History museum would enthral, but the visit had been far from a success. Alex and Lucinda had rampaged through South Kensington almost uncontrollably; tempers had escalated as a result of the crowds and the temperature… If he were to come back with Marita, Toby decides they would come alone, just the two of them. So sadly not for a while then. Another slice of the future which now seems a little foggier than before.

Inwardly he curses his Achilles, his luck. If it hadn't snapped then he would still be playing cricket - including that return fixture against Bourden where the team had exacted their revenge! And he wouldn't have needed to come to London in the first place, nor been burdened with crutches, this walk, these sudden thoughts.

~

Imogen finds the pulse of activity on the street mesmerising: pedestrians, cars, cyclists, buses. The rhythm in the throng is a mirror of what she has already seen elsewhere: at King's Cross, on the tube, near St. Thomas's. And then she notices how many joggers there seem to be - not that Borough High Street strikes her as ideal running territory given the need to constantly veer around pedestrians and weave in and out of traffic. As she lifts her coffee, she wonders if it is like this all across London, the dedicated and lycra-clad doing what they can to keep in shape. Imogen has never been a runner. During her sporadic visits to the gym she steered clear of treadmills, preferring the less aerobic exercise mat and a few light weights. But having said that, she has largely steered clear of the gym altogether. Taking advantage of a hefty work-sponsored discount on the membership fee was one thing, but making use of it something else entirely. Her attendance seemed to go in pulses, triggered by haphazardly related events such as birthdays, year ends, the need to be able to fit into a dress for a wedding or party, or the virtual needle on her bathroom weighing machine trespassing into 'red' territory. Although there was much about working-out which appealed to her - the ability to construct a regime, plan sequences of exercises, give herself targets - Imogen found she lacked the dedication to see any of them through to conclusion. It was less an issue of discipline and more one of application. Interestingly, with dieting it seemed to be the other way round, application defeated by discipline: she could apply herself to the cooking, the shopping, but never had the strength of character to stick with it. There was always something tastier in the cupboard calling to her. Perhaps they were one and the same thing, discipline and application, but she wasn't sure - and then such recognition suddenly strikes her as a point of danger: what if one of the interviewers asked her about self-imposed disciplines at work, or how she applied herself to a problem? Placing her cup down in front of her, she tries to resolve this particular conundrum, seeing if she can settle on suitable definitions and their associated experiences in readiness for an as yet unasked question. She watches a man in purple leggings and a bright orange vest as he sprints into and out of view on the other side of the road. Did he offer her a parallel she could use? Discipline, the mental strength to get himself ready to go out running; application, how hard he tried once he was on the road. Could she make that work? She glances at her watch. Eleven-thirty. Time to finish up then return along St. Thomas' Road.

"I'm here for an interview with Alistair Burgess."

The uniformed woman at the reception desk smiles up at her.

"Your name?"

"Imogen Mansfield."

As the receptionist consults the screen in front of her, Imogen is reminded of how much she hates her name. The 'Imogen' part is fine; it has a certain class, and benefits from being impossible to shorten in any meaningful way. Her sisters - who seemed entirely happy to be called 'Lou' and 'Em' - had tried to reduce her to 'Im', but it wouldn't stick. What they *had* managed to do for themselves, of course, was change their surnames. Of the two, Emma's new name is by far the superior, layered with the suggestion that it possesses a certain romanticism if spoken with the hint of a European accent. But neither of them are a Mansfield any more, and it's that to which Imogen objects the most. It is a name with connotations. Although she has never been there, she imagines it to be an unattractive run-down kind of place, not far enough north to be truly interesting. It is surely small, undistinguished, middle-of-the-road; and she has always worried that when people hear the word - just as the receptionist has done now - they will inevitably draw parallels between Imogen and the place of the same name. When the woman across the desk looks up and hands Imogen a badge, does she do so seeing her for who she is or does she unavoidably see someone who is likely to be a human incarnation of Mansfield the place?

"Wear this at all times, please." She waves her hand toward the other side of the atrium. "If you'd like to make your way through security, someone will then show you where to go."

Turning her back on the woman, Imogen heads across the foyer still playing with names and wondering about their relationship to place. Do people make assumptions about Stevenage too, and if so, might they also rub off on her? She has heard that in many quarters it is seen as a 'new town' and somehow less significant because of that; a plastic and antiseptic kind of place beaten only by Milton Keynes in a race to the bottom. Hardly a ringing endorsement - either of the place or those living there. But London? Ah, here the world is surely your oyster and you can be anything you want!

Security looks as if it has been stolen from an airport. There is a conveyor belt attached to a large machine in order to scan baggage, and an x-ray arch through which visitors have to walk. She places her bag on the belt and joins the short queue for the arch. Once the other side, she finds her bag resting on a long table; a uniformed man has one hand on it.

"Your bag, madam?" He smiles as she approaches.

"Yes."

"May I?" He motions to open it. "Just a precaution."

"Of course."

There is nothing of any note inside: lipstick, purse, compact, phone, handkerchief, a folded copy of her cv, a pen, and a small notebook in which she has written potential questions and candidate answers. His examination of the contents is over in a moment.

"Thank you Ms Mansfield," the man says after a glance at her badge. "If you'd like to walk round the corner to the lifts, someone will direct you."

That name again. As she moves on she thinks again of her siblings and how she had always assumed that, like them, marriage would change her name. One marries for love of course, as both Louise and Emma had done - twice in Louise's case - and for a while Imogen herself had been able to play with a prospective new name. While neither exotic or particularly interesting, 'Imogen Rodwell' would have done well enough. For a time - for some considerable time - she had assumed Sam was on the verge of proposing to her. In readiness she had even taken to trying out her new signature. But Sam abandoned the field - or fell at the final hurdle, depending on your point of view - and in doing so taken his name with him. For a while she had been heartbroken.

"Ms Mansfield." This time she was being addressed by a tall slim woman, heavily made-up, and with the lilt of a southern Irish accent. "Floor seventeen, I see."

Imogen glances down to the badge which has adorned her lapel since she left the reception desk and notes the emboldened '17' in its bottom right-hand corner. She is disappointed the interview isn't being held higher up in the building.

The Irish woman glances to a bank of lifts.

"The lift second from the end on your right should be next. Once inside, just place your badge against the pad and press seventeen. When you get there please go straight to reception."

Another reception, Imogen thinks. It will have taken four people to get her into a building merely for her to still be waiting to be called into an interview. She can't imagine such a process in Stevenage - and wonders whether Mansfield, the town, would have or need any security at all.

When she steps out of the lift a minute or so later she is greeted by a sign displaying the names of the companies occupying that floor and thus instruction as to whether she should turn left or right to find them. There are just three names, and only one - the one she is interested in - leads off to the left. Imogen walks past the other lifts, both male and female toilets, and through a heavy set of double doors. A large desk, shaped in the form of a gentle crescent, awaits her. One of the two women behind it looks up. As she approaches, Imogen can't help but notice the luxury feel of the carpeting, the company's name in a super-large font on a panel behind the desk, its two-tone brand everywhere.

"Ms Mansfield," the woman says, her tone vaguely familiar, as if they had previously met.

"Yes. Hello."

"Thank you for being so prompt. Alastair and Anthony will be a few minutes, but let me show you to the room so that you can get settled." She stands up and comes to Imogen's side. "This way please."

They walk along a short but generous corridor, meeting rooms on either side. Just before another set of double doors, the woman indicates a room to her right, and ushers Imogen inside. Not especially large, the room is dominated by two tables set to form a square, two chairs tucked underneath each of the four resulting sides. Against another brand-encrusted wall a low cabinet plays host to bottles of water, glasses, a pot of mints.

"Would you like a tea or coffee?"

"Water will be just fine, thank you."

"Then please help yourself; they won't be long." And then, just as she is about to leave the room: "And relax, they won't bite! Perhaps admire the view while you're waiting."

In terms of quality, the meeting room and its contents are a cut above those with which she is familiar - and the view most certainly has nothing in common with Stevenage! Below and to her left is London Bridge station. Imogen is struck by the size of it, the number of platforms; and along the multitude of tracks it seems as if most are hosting trains moving, arriving and departing. She undertakes a quick count. Seven or eight, at least. And then beyond, London's east graduates away to the horizon, and she is struck by its size, how far it reaches. For a moment she does not move, then turning back into the room recognises that she needs to choose where to sit. Given the room is not laid out in conventional interview format, perhaps this is the first test. She settles on a chair on the side closest to the cabinet, one which gives her a view of both the door and the vista outside. Placing her handbag on it, she pours herself a glass of water and then stands again at the window. Mesmerised, she allows London to absorb her for a few minutes before she checks her watch. Still five minutes to go. She glances over her shoulder to the door. Soon she will hear her name spoken again and she will endeavour not to cringe.

Geographically, she is as far from her professional Stevenage life as it is possible to be: standing at a window around a fifth of the way up The Shard, enveloped in the surroundings of an entirely different company, and about to put herself on the line. Right now she is no longer Imogen Mansfield; she feels as if she is on the verge of a transition that will change her life, a thought which also succeeds in suggesting parallels between professional and personal. She may soon cease to be 'Imogen, the PA from Stevenage' and become 'Imogen, the EA in London'. Or, if needs be, a PA. Yet she will still be 'a Mansfield'. Ever since the reception desk downstairs, her name has clung to her. For a moment she fantasises about her being the interviewer, the candidates being potential suitors all vying to succeed in being the one to liberate her from her name. As much as she wants someone to give her a new professional role - here, today - she has ambitions to appoint someone herself, a knight in shining armour who is called something other than 'Mansfield'.

Is that what this is all about? Not just the interview, but the place? She looks out across the massive metropolis and is shaken by the thought that just possibly, somewhere out there - or even in the building in which she now stands! - is that special someone she needs to find so that she can offer them the task of changing her, both name and person. London: more than where this job and building happens to be; it is a place where everything is possible. She is suddenly daunted.

~

"Lawrence."

So not 'Larry' then.

He imagined there would be no issue in recognising his brother, yet finds himself disappointed that nothing seems changed about him: no scars or new blemishes, no flash of white hair. Dylan had always been lucky with his hair.

"Tessa?" he enquires, finding Dylan alone.

"In the ladies. We met at Waterloo and walked here together. She won't be a minute."

Lawrence is suddenly glad he took the Embankment option. Glancing down at the table, he sees Tessa's bag slung over the back of the chair to Dylan's left. Given it is a table set for four, he has the choice of taking the free place next to Dylan or that next to Tessa. Perhaps above anything else choosing where to sit is as much a statement about who he doesn't want to be next to. Whether or not convention suggests he should choose the seat alongside Dylan, Lawrence does not, preferring to be across from him and beside Tessa. If he requires an ally at any point over the next hour or so, history tells him Tessa is the one most likely to fill that role. Dylan, the eldest of them, had always been his nemesis, once locking him in the cupboard at the top of the stairs for half an hour as punishment for daring to play with one of his toys. Superior both physically and intellectually, he had ensured Lawrence was always kept in his place - a pecking order which became even easier to enforce when their father left.

"You're looking well," Dylan offers flatly.

Lawrence is about to reply when he sees Tessa approaching. He stands to greet her, as much out of shock as politeness: not only has his sister seemingly felt the full weight of the last two years, but it is as if she has taken on others' share too. Dylan's perhaps, as if she had become his Dorian Gray painting. For an instant he wonders if she inadvertently accepted a slice of his own burden too, but then dismisses the notion. Her hair is greyer, her face worn, and in the way she moves, sits, tries an exploratory smile, Lawrence finds it hard to believe it is not she who is the senior party.

"Good journey?"

They spend the next few minutes engaged in inconsequential talk about trains, the weather - and a little about London too. They order coffee - cappuccino for Dylan, Americano for Tessa, latte for him - and both Dylan and Tessa choose cake from the menu. It is only after their order is fulfilled and Dylan has taken the first forkful of his lemon drizzle that the conversation really begins.

"So," he says, mouth empty but the fork still poised in his hand, "how do you want to do this? It's your call, Lawrence."

He finds his name both a barrier and a measure. If he can get Dylan to succumb to 'Larry' just once before he leaves, perhaps that will be the proof of something. The absence of a plan strikes him again.

"Yes." He hesitates, sensing the few words he may have rehearsed already evaporating. Nearby, the slowly turning ferris wheel encroaches on his peripheral vision. "Thanks for coming. I mean, agreeing to meet. I daresay my request came a bit out of the blue."

"You might say that." Dylan stabs another portion of his cake, the way he brings it to his mouth the embodiment of challenge.

"We talked about it. Obviously." Tessa's tone is slightly more conciliatory. "I mean, how could we not? And I don't think we were ever going to say 'no'." She shoots Dylan a glance which Lawrence cannot miss. "So that was never a real question."

"What was the question" - having divested his fork of cake and absorbed the morsel in two chews, Dylan picks up the thread - "is why? Why now? And after all this time?"

"We wondered - I wondered - if there was something wrong. Or if there was news; something you needed us to know."

Lawrence is about to respond to his sister when Dylan interjects.

"If you've heard anything about the old man, then we're simply not interested. Not after what he did. I thought we'd made our position on him crystal clear."

As he listens, Lawrence finds himself parsing his brother's words slightly differently: "not after what *you* did", "our position on *you* crystal clear".

"No, I've heard nothing about him; and I daresay my attitude towards him isn't that far removed from yours." Including them both in his gaze as he speaks, he tries to suggest common ground. "And as for anything wrong, Tess, no, nothing like that." Lawrence tries a sip of his coffee but it is too hot to drink. He replaces the mug on the table. "Not in any major way; I mean, I'm not ill or anything." Looking at Dylan, for a moment he wishes he might have been. It would be easier if there was something concrete he could leverage or use to garner sympathy; it might tilt things in his favour. He thinks of God's abandonment of him. Even if that were concrete, how might he unwrap it for them?

"So?" Dylan, between forkfuls, renews his challenge.

"I suppose I felt it was time to set the record straight. From my perspective, I mean." He hesitates again. "You know what happened - or at least you think you do - but perhaps I understand it better now myself. Perhaps because I've had time enough (and all of that time on my own) to understand why I did what I did. Or didn't do... This is difficult... Maybe I felt I needed to try and replay things. Or try and find something I'd lost."

"Us?" Tessa suggests.

Lawrence had never considered his siblings as lost to him, not in the sense of how his mother was lost to him. Or God. They had deliberately chosen not to understand how uniquely difficult their mother's death had been for him, and in doing so had raised a drawbridge against him. He has never regarded his exile as voluntary but rather their doing, and so any notion of 'losing' them seems to him to be looking at history through the wrong end of the lens.

"Yes," he says in spite of his analysis, at which Dylan shifts a little in his seat. Lawrence knows his brother wants a full-fledged apology, wants him to grovel before he'll concede any ground. In recognising as much, he also sees that if he were inclined to be inflexible about it, aggressive even in denying Dylan the satisfaction of such a climb-down, then this might be the moment for him to stand up and walk out. Spoken or otherwise, Dylan's terms for filial reengagement are patently obvious, and if Lawrence chooses to remain, to try and explain, then he will not be doing so against his own agenda. He looks at his sister whose attention is momentary diverted by the crash of a plate elsewhere in the restaurant; the cake in front of her remains untouched. He will talk to them both, but he will speak to Tessa.

"I never ceased to love her. Mum, I mean. Never." He starts with a fact. "I know you might have drawn a parallel between me and dad, but there never was one. Not really. He left because he didn't want her last days dragging him down, interfering with his life. I" - he pauses to find a word - "absented myself for completely the opposite reason."

"You didn't want *your* life dragging *her* down!" Dylan is incredulous.

"No, no. Not that. Never that." In spite of his profession, his love of words, Lawrence finds them deserting him. "That's not what I meant. Of course, not. I just thought… I so didn't want her to die, I thought that maybe if I wasn't there, couldn't see it, wasn't party to her illness, then somehow it wouldn't be real. That she would get better. There'd be a miracle. Everything would be fine."

"You believed that?" Another short laugh escapes his brother's lips.

"Yes. I think I did. If I was there, tending to her, being a witness if you like, then I would be endorsing what was happening to her. As if I would be giving her illness permission to eat away at her; to take her from me. From us."

"But she needed looking after," Tessa's observation is delivered softly, as if she might have been talking to a child.

"I know that. I mean, I know that now; but then I hoped it wasn't really the case."

"And you left us to put in the hard yards, Lawrence. To be 'witness', as you put it. Tessa and I. When there should have been three sharing the load - or four - there was just the two of us. Fifty-fifty, more or less." Dylan looks to Tessa whose eyes are fixed on her untouched cake. "And God knows we tried to get you to take on your fair share. But in the end... Well."

And from Lawrence's perspective God did know. Was his reluctance to contribute to his mother's final weeks of care where he began to earn His disfavour, if that's what it was? Were those the first black marks which eventually accumulated sufficiently for God to up-sticks on him too? There was no miracle after all. He looks at Tessa.

"Don't you think I know that now? Even if I chose not to see it then, Tessa. You've no idea the remorse I felt when she died, how torn apart I was by missing so many chances to be with her before she went. But I was twisted inside-out by this ridiculous notion I had. I didn't want it to be real - and I thought I could undo it all, make it right..." There is a pause. Lawrence tries his coffee again, this time taking two long sips. "That's what I came to realise, have come to see. I was blinded by my fear."

"Your fear?" Tessa again.

"Of losing her. And in doing so, losing myself I suppose."

"Are we supposed to feel sorry for you?" Dylan asks. "You were as selfish as the old man; plain and simple."

"I'm not sure that's entirely fair," Tessa says.

"Not selfish?" Incredulity again. "And now he wants, what, to be forgiven? For us to say that we understand?"

Both are questions Lawrence has asked himself. They have different answers.

"Beginning to understanding - to try to understand - would be a start," he agrees, knowing forgiveness rests in other hands entirely. "It would be something. Or if not understanding, then at least acknowledgement."

"Of what?"

"My admitting that I was wrong - and perhaps that my motives were benevolent and not selfish."

"The first part is easy," Tessa leans slightly towards him.

"But the second…?" Dylan lets the words hang between them over his empty plate - and Tessa's full one.

Silence cocoons them. Elsewhere, chatter from other tables continues unabated, a choral work backed by the chiming of cutlery on crockery, a kind of percussive accompaniment. Draining his coffee, Lawrence sees his sister sip again at hers; soon it will surely be too cold to drink. He catches Dylan glance at the untouched cake on her plate and can imagine him taking offence at her indecisiveness, the waste of it. As far as he can recall, there had never been a time when Dylan hadn't been upset by something.

Neither of them are looking at him. He has opened himself up to them as best he can, confessed his guilt, but it is clearly not enough - at least for Dylan. But was anything ever going to be enough? Even though he senses he has made progress with Tessa, Lawrence wonders if this whole escapade hasn't been a mistake. He tries to find in his sister's eyes a trace of the softness he had loved as a child, but all he can see reflected is the pain of a middle-aged woman.

"Before she died," he drags them back, forces them to abandon their gazing across the café, out of the window, "I turned to God." It is a word he knows not even Dylan can take issue with. "I'd never been that way inclined. Of course none of us were, given mum and dad weren't like that. Perhaps He was the only thing I could think of that might help save her. A last throw of the dice, if you like. It was a desperate attempt. I mean, you hear things don't you? Not that I believed in miracles, but sometimes… So I tried. In my own amateur way I prayed; I tried to find… I don't know what really. If there was something there, a benevolence; then perhaps… Of course, it didn't make any difference. No prayers were answered, no miracles were forthcoming. She died, you and I stopped talking. It was almost the opposite of what I'd asked for."

"I didn't know," Tessa's tone betraying her feeling that she had just been let in on a secret.

"Why should you? How could you?" Lawrence tries to give her a reassuring smile before looking up at Dylan who sits mute and unresponsive across the table, a man suddenly out of his comfort zone. "When mum died I thought that was it. I mean I stopped praying - after all I no longer had any reason to do so. I'd placed all my chips on red and watched the ball land in black. That was how it felt. She was gone - *you* were both gone - and I was suddenly alone for the first time in my life. Oh I had my work, of course; I went back to Lincoln, threw myself into it. That was some consolation I suppose. I read more, tried to invent things to do outside all that, to keep me occupied… But it was soon a desolate kind of existence. I thought of getting in touch with you then, but I knew it was too soon, all too raw." He scans their faces; Tessa's intent on his, Dylan's impassive. "And then I heard this voice." Almost imperceptibly, Dylan raises an eyebrow. "Not a voice, of course, but something like that. Talking to me. It was helpful, reassuring - and when you've nothing else… Any port in a storm, isn't that what they say?" Tessa moves her hand across the table, part-way toward his own. Lawrence stares at it for a moment. "It was comforting, helpful; a kind of confessor. And although I imagined it as a masculine voice, I used to pretend that it was mum talking to me - or the father we'd wanted but never had. Someone who could help me through those dark days."

"And you thought that was God?" There is an strange ambiguity in Dylan's tone which Lawrence is unable to unwrap.

"For me, yes."

"But does it matter what it was?" Tessa's question is aimed at her elder brother. "Isn't the important thing the strength it gave Larry when he was struggling?"

Dylan shrugs his shoulders.

"Remember that boy in your year at school? Francis, I think his name was." Lawrence looks at Dylan. "He had an imaginary friend didn't he? Well it was probably little bit like that."

"But he was a nutcase! A complete fruit cake!" Dylan glances again to his sister's plate. "He went away after a couple of years; none of us knew where."

"I expect his family just moved," said Tessa, the hand she had edged toward Lawrence's own now toying with her fork.

"Whatever," said Lawrence, not wishing to lose the thread. "But this voice was a little bit like an imaginary friend for me. In a good way. It didn't feel crazy; it didn't feel weird. It was proof that I hadn't been deserted, that God had been listening. I wondered if - having been unable to do anything about mum - He might have decided He could help me."

"So what happened?" Tessa teases a morsel of cake onto her fork.

"Things got better. I stabilised - for the want of a better word. I settled back into my work, my routine life. I gradually reconciled myself to what had happened. It took some time - about a year maybe. I thought of you both."

"God told you to speak to us?"

Lawrence ignores his brother's question.

"Then, about three months ago, the voice just stopped. One day I woke up and it wasn't there. I was distraught; I hadn't realised how much I'd come to rely on it. It was as if God had moved on, had enough of me. And I didn't know why. First mum, then the two of you," he pauses for a reaction but there is none, "and suddenly God too. If I'd felt alone after mum died, this new abandonment was so total: sudden, bleak, somehow conclusive. Where could I turn after I'd been abandoned so absolutely?" He swallows to clear his throat. "So no, Dylan; God didn't tell me to try and speak to you. In a way it was completely the opposite."

Taking his turn to look out onto London, Lawrence watches the Eye as it makes its pedestrian progress to nowhere, and he wonders if that isn't a reflection of their meeting. The concrete which surrounds him - the tables, chairs, cutlery, crockery - are all insignificant; importance is buried in elements that remain untouchable: emotions, attitudes, thoughts and feelings. Life would surely be easier if the later were capable of being manifested physically. Back on Tessa's plate he notices the absence of a small chunk of cake and wants that to mean something.

"Miss."

Dylan's voice drags him back. A waitress appears.

"Another cappuccino for me. Sis?" Tessa shakes her head. "Lawrence?"

"Latte. Thanks."

Is Dylan's offer important? Lawrence wishes he knew.

"So where are you now?"

He looks at Tessa.

"Where am I?"

"Emotionally, I mean. Or at least I think I do."

"I suspect my answer may be as vague as your question, Tess." He smiles as best he can. "Alone? Searching?"

"Still praying?" she asks.

"Not that I'm aware."

"Maybe you should try." Tessa looks to Dylan for support just as his attention is focussed on their waitress heading towards their table from the far side of the café. There is a short hiatus as new coffee cups replace old and the appropriate pleasantries exchanged. "You never know," Tessa continues as soon as the waitress is out of earshot, "it might not be too late."

"Too late for what?" asks Dylan as he stirs his cappuccino, a slight distaste in his voice. "Isn't this just life? Make you own bed and all that."

"You'll be telling Larry to 'pull himself together' in a minute; that or some such nonsense."

"And why not?" Momentarily focussed on Tessa, Dylan speaks as if Lawrence isn't there. "Wasn't that what we had to do after mum died - get on with things? Go back to our lives, an existence without her? It didn't matter how much we missed her or loved her, she wasn't going to be there any more. Fact." He pauses just a second. "I'm sorry to be so black-and-white about it, but isn't that just how things are? There was no impact when the old man ran off - at least as far as I could see - and I know mum's going was different, but even so..."

"You forget one thing, Dylan."

"Oh?" He looks at Tessa.

"Whether we'd want to admit it or not, Larry was always closer to mum than we were. And probably vice versa, if I'm honest. He was always going to be hit harder by her dying. We had other things, other people to fall back on..."

Knowing it cannot be countered, Lawrence waits for his brother to respond to Tessa's challenge. He turns the clock back two years and reimagines the funeral, Dylan in the front row with Sarah and Connie, the little girl sobbing at the thought of never seeing her favourite granny again. And Tessa trying desperately not to crumble, propped up by Penny, the two of them leaving the church arm-in-arm looking more like sisters than lovers. He realises the gap between them is not just about his lack of interaction but the dearth of knowledge too. As he looks at Tessa he cannot help but see things have also been hard for her since they were last together - and not because of their mother or God. Feeling the need to catch-up, to divert attention away from himself, to see if there is another route to reconnecting with them, he turns to Dylan.

"How is Sarah? And Connie; she must be, what, eight now?"

"Nine."

It is a cue for Dylan to fall into a potted history of his last two years: trials and tribulations at work, trials and tribulations at home. He had sidestepped a round of redundancies, and Sarah had swerved a breast cancer scare. Lawrence feels the latter is the most important of the two, but remains unsure Dylan sees things in precisely the same way; perhaps for him they are on a par. When he wraps-up his précis with a claim that "it is what it is", Lawrence is struck not by any sense of defeatism but rather abdication, as if Dylan is content not to take responsibility for what happens to him. He thinks back two years and tries to draw parallels with his own attitude as far as his mother's care was concerned. There is nothing soft-edged in Dylan's exposition, and even pressing him for more on Connie uncovers nothing.

"And you, Sis?"

Tessa laughs, a certain nervousness blended with a hint of irrelevance. Though not the youngest of the three, Lawrence remembers swathes of their growing-up when she was the passive one, happy to acquiesce, tag along. Perhaps such behaviour was the natural corollary to Dylan's bullying; perhaps she had already been sufficiently brow-beaten by the time Dylan turned his attention to his baby brother.

When nothing follows the laugh, Lawrence re-prompts her.

"How's Penny?"

Dylan glances at his sister, then raises his coffee to his lips. He says nothing.

"Penny is no more," Tessa says - then realising what she has just implied, quickly clarifies: "I mean, she's fine. At least as far a I know. We split-up about four months after mum's funeral."

"I'm sorry."

"No need to be." She tries a smile; looks down at her cake as if the fork in her hand is alien. "It hadn't been working for a while really; at least that's how it seems on reflection. There was no big climax or denouement; we both woke up one day and knew it was over. That's all. It is what it is, as Dylan said."

"And since then?"

Tessa shakes her head a little. Looks out of the window. Her words seem prompted by the ferris wheel.

"Same old, same old. Bit like you and Dylan really. You know: work, grind, work, grind. There's been no-one else - in case that's what you're wondering. I'm not sure I'm up to all that palaver, at least not at the moment. And no God, no voices either." She tries another laugh. "Though that does sound quite appealing."

The downbeat cadence to her voice ushers in another silence. They each focus on what sits in front of them on the table: Dylan attacks his cappuccino, Tessa admits defeat as far as her cake is concerned. And Lawrence watches both as he gradually drains his latte, trying to reestablish exactly who the two people sitting across from him really are. Does he even recognise them from his past? Can he make that link? And, if so, does he like them now more or less than he did back then?

"So," Dylan returns his empty cup theatrically to the table, "what happens now - other than I pay the bill and we each go our separate ways?"

They both look at Lawrence.

"Was that - useful?" Tessa asks. "I mean, it was good to see you Larry, to know you're still in one piece."

"Likewise." Lawrence smiles at his sister. "It's been too long - and I know that's all my fault, but there you have it. I won't repeat Dylan's catch-phrase…"

For a split second Dylan thinks of smiling, a notion betrayed by his the twitch of a muscle or two in his face. Perhaps he believes his brother's statement credits him with the last word, or that he has furnished them with the 'best' words, the most appropriate ones. But instead of that he raises a hand to attract the attention of a waitress.

"So, has it helped?" Tessa prompts again, dragging Lawrence back from staring at Dylan's hand.

"Helped?" They both look at him. "I think so. I mean, how can it not have?" He pauses. "In terms of what happens next? In micro terms I'm going to walk along the river for a while and then head back to King's Cross for my train home."

"And in macro terms?"

"Ah." Lawrence looks at the Eye. "Just keep buggering on, I suppose. Hope that something positive happens. Isn't that what everyone does?"

"Well in any event, this was good," Tessa's hand finally makes it across the table to his arm. "And overdue." She looks at Dylan, his attention is back with them now that someone is heading their way with a credit card machine.

"It would be churlish to disagree," he admits.

And then within minutes they are outside and separated. Lawrence had shaken Dylan's hand once again, and the hug offered him by Tessa seemed, above all else, to demonstrate just how thin she had become. He watches them walk away between walls of concrete as they head back to Waterloo together, and then turns to face the Thames. To his left the Eye continues its slow spin, and on the river various craft plough east and west. He tries to assess the state of the tide, to see if he can discern where it is in its cycle, but to his untrained eye the evidence is inconclusive.

~

"Tilt," Duncan says, turning and lowering his arm in one combined motion, "there you are."

I look into the café to see if there's anyone I recognise - or, more obscurely, if I can spot someone who looks like the kind of individual Duncan might know. From about half-way back, Justin Pawson, his own hand still raised, smiles our way. It looks as if he's trying to flag down a bus - or get permission to go to the toilet.

"Justin," I say - admittedly unnecessarily - aiming the word at Duncan and intending to follow it up with something about coincidence.

"I've asked him to join us," Duncan interrupts, "kill two birds with one stone," and begins to follow the waitress to the table where Justin is already standing, his hand now proffered in greeting.

Where I trust Duncan about as much as any writer should trust their agent, Justin's a different kettle of fish. He is too smooth by far. You could lift him and his pin-stripe suit, his slightly gaudy tie, his black brogues - *black* brogues! - and deposit him in any number of places and he'd appear reasonably at home: a bank, an insurance company, a classy travel company. But publishing? I've never been convinced. However Duncan rates him, which I suppose is what matters most; and thus far he is on-track to deliver what he's promised. I try to work out if I'm in the mood to cut him some slack. "At ease, Tilt; at ease!"

"Justin," I say again (once more unnecessarily) taking his hand and then subsequently resisting the temptation to wipe my own on my trousers, "this is a surprise." I leave out the word 'nice' with sufficient clumsiness to try and ensure its absence registers.

"Duncan told me you two were meeting. Seemed like a good opportunity to gatecrash and talk about books and things."

Given the level of Justin's conversation around books is passable at best - in spite of his chosen profession! - I wonder how he'll fare with 'things'. We sit. The waitress immediately presents us with menus and asks about drinks. Justin says something about the sun and the yardarm, trying to be funny.

I order a black Americano. There is idle chit-chat as we glance through the menu. It being too early for lunch (as well as alcohol) the only options seem to be cake or pastries. Or abstinence. When both Duncan and Justin choose Lemon Drizzle I make a point of declining. "I have an appointment in a little while for lunch," I fib, encouraging the notion that this being one of my relatively infrequent forays from York to London I am - not unreasonably - a man in demand.

Justin looks at Duncan who, surprisingly, still seems on edge.

"Well," Duncan says, "then we'd better crack on. Don't want to hold you up."

It seems my white lie will also serve to minimise the time I have to spend in Justin's company. I smile dutifully and glance in his direction, noticing the slight stain on the lapel of his jacket, and the interior label which confesses to a somewhat inferior brand of High Street tailor. Without so much as a glance, I settle a little deeper into my tweed's satin-pink lining. You can tell a lot about someone from what they wear and how they wear it. Most people make the mistake of merely equating clothes with money, the lazy conclusion being that the better the clothes the deeper the pockets. "Tilt, Old Boy, that's pretty good! You must remember to use it somewhere!" I smile and slip my hand into one of my inner jacket pockets and retrieve a small notebook and pen.

"Just had a thought," I deliberately look at Duncan first. "Can't afford to lose it."

"Always working, eh?" Justin's smile is almost a smirk, and I wonder if that's his first trespass away from books and into 'things'. Not that he's wrong, of course. I *am* always working; that's the curse isn't it?

Having scribbled the line, I replace the notebook. Justin and Duncan are whispering across from me. It's all vaguely conspiratorial. I wonder if they've been comparing notes. I cough (a little theatrically I must admit) and bring them back to me.

"Yes," Duncan reorients himself. "Where were we?" - and I think to myself "nowhere yet, Duncan; nowhere" - "So. The thing is that the Adelphi want to modify the length of *The Colour of Rust*'s run."

"You tell me when a theatre manager didn't want something or other!" I relax into what feels like familiar territory. It was the same with the Shaw, and more so later on as I began to gain a foothold in the capital. The critics even started associating the word 'gold' with my plays, so why wouldn't impresarios want more?

"Maybe so, but the Adelphi actually wants to cut it."

I stare at Duncan's mouth, unable to believe the words he has just uttered have escaped from there. I've never heard him say anything like that; indeed, I've never heard anyone say anything so ridiculous. Off my guard and forced onto new ground, I look at Justin expecting to see a broad smile on his face, to hear a laugh escape, a confession that *this* is the joke they have concocted in order to wind me up. But his face is somewhat stoney.

"Bookings have been down," Duncan continues speaking to the side of my face. "Very disappointing. It appears people have read the reviews and are believing them."

"People?" I must have either looked or sounded incredulous when I returned my gaze to Duncan.

"Tell me you've read the reviews?" There is a note of pleading in his voice.

I can't help but laugh.

"Reviews?" I try and bluff my way into letting them think I find the very idea of reviews an alien concept. "Of course. Some. I mean, a few in the beginning."

"They weren't kind," Justin offers, stage right. I ignore him; this isn't his territory after all.

"There are always negative reviews, Duncan. Even *Dining at the Dorchester* had its detractors."

"Yes, but they were in the minority. This time…" He pauses. Now understanding the reason for of his being on edge earlier, I find some it being transferred to me. It is an unwelcome visitor. I don't do nervousness.

"This time?" I quote back at him with all the confidence and superiority I can muster.

"I admit in the beginning it was a mixed bag." He offers, searching for some middle-ground. "Some people said some good things. But it's become a bit of a bone for some of the hacks, Tilt; almost as if it's an opportunity for them to settle a score."

"Jealousy; that's all it is." I laugh. "Envy of talent." I look briefly at Justin then back to Duncan.

"But they're not letting it go… Even *The Standard*…" Duncan takes refuge in a sip of coffee. I hear Justin's fork on his plate as he attacks his lemon drizzle. "The Adelphi say they were two-thirds empty last night. And it's looking worse. They want to close after Saturday."

It's a good job I'm not mid-way through picking up my own coffee. What is going on? Duncan is either speaking in a coded language no-one has taught me how to translate, or has invited the wrong person to the meeting.

"Close? I never close early. Three months, minimum. Three months, Duncan - not three fucking weeks! Surely it's the post-Covid effect. Isn't everyone suffering?"

"They say they've factored that in. Generally they'd expect to be about ten percent down at worst. That's the norm across the city. Not nearly forty percent."

I bat the numbers away.

"There's nothing wrong with *Rust*. Nothing. Yes, it may be a little off-point in terms of my usual work, but I thought it about time I got a little more serious. I'm sure we talked about that way back?"

"We did; but only in vague generalities."

I ignore his implication. My dander is up.

"So then, that's what *Rust* is. I'm sorry if it strays a little too far from the banal 'careful there, Vicar!' the sainted but limited critics are comfortable with. And if it's playing havoc with the Adelphi's statistics... You know I was never happy with them casting that young chap as Rodri. I mean, he's still mortally tarnished by the abysmal failure of that police thing he did for ITV, so what did they expect? Sod it, Duncan, he's hardly Olivier."

It is, I feel, a blow impeccably delivered; one which is impossible to counter. Looking at Justin for support - not that I really need it, you understand - I find him nodding, trying to look wise. Something which doesn't sit well with that suit of his.

"You may be right," Duncan concedes, "but it's not just that, is it?"

"Not just what?" I wish people could speak more clearly, say what they mean. It's all very well for my characters to indulge in the odd moment of hyperbole for dramatic effect, but now's not the time.

"The numbers weren't so good for *Dining at the Dorchester*. Not compared to the first three."

"Stellar," I suggest, knowing that one word is enough to encapsulate those early triumphs.

"But damn it, Tilt, the Adelphi have a clause... They're closing after Saturday and there's nothing we can do about it."

I notice Duncan hasn't touched his cake. Seeing the direction of my gaze he looks down at it too, then, almost with an air of guilt, picks up his fork. It will, I conclude, give him an excuse not to say anything for a few minutes.

"So that's it, is it?" Unable to face relative silence - the heavy pause of him eating, Justin dumb, the general hubbub around us - I march into the breech. "Take the money and run. Is that what you're saying? Consign *Rust* to the bin and go back to writing the sort of stuff 'people' loved ten years ago?"

"Not exactly." Justin's voice drags me away from my contemplation of Duncan's fork on its journey to his mouth.

"'Not exactly' what?"

Justin tries a smile, as if he's a naughty schoolboy who has just committed a minor faux pas.

"Sorry. What I should have said is 'not entirely'." Seeing me about to interrupt, he pushes on. "Obviously I didn't need to be here for Duncan to tell you about the Adelphi and all that. Indeed, you're probably wondering what I'm doing here - or if my presence has anything to do with you at all."

"It crossed my mind." I tried to deliver the line so that it sounded like "it was the first thing that occurred to me".

Nodding, Justin acknowledges both the words if not their meaning. Point made, I feel happy enough to take a sip of my coffee. It is now too cool. I will need to drink it down quickly or let it go. Remembering who paid for it, I try and weight up where the greater insult will reside - then drink it down anyway.

"It's about the book."

"Oh?" If Justin thinks he has drawn a connection between the Adelphi and the collection of my work he is planning to publish, then he is much mistaken. I notice the stain on his jacket once again and reflect how 'stain' and 'satin' are anagrams of each other; just swap two letters round... The difference between people in such minutiae.

"Given what's happened with *Rust*, we don't feel that now's the right time to be putting the book out. We'll be swimming against the tide, as it were." He tries to look smug at his clever metaphor.

"'Swimming'..." I laugh, in spite of myself. I hope it is an ironic or pitying laugh. "Justin, the plays are as good today as they were yesterday; none of that's changed. And no matter what the critics or the bloody Adelphi say, *Rust* is a good piece of work. It may be my best."

I deliver the last line as a boxer might attempt to land his signature punch; the uppercut which will send his hapless opponent bouncing onto the rope and then back into the centre of the ring only to be floored by a straight right.

But Justin - shit suit and all - sways out of the way.

"That may be, but without sentiment on our side I don't think we'll sell." He pauses, clearly unfinished. "The plan was simple: *Rust* is a huge success; *Rust* generates the interest; *Rust* is the headline act in a collected works. Simple. Easy sell. It would have been a triumph."

"'Would have been'?" I hate myself for echoing back what he has said and turning it into a question. Such laziness is fine for characters in a play - especially those with limited imaginations - but it hardly becomes me. But I let it go. I have to. "Steady, Tilt Old Boy!"

"Indeed. Because *Rust* has not been a success the whole premise falls away." As Justin leans forward I am conscious of Duncan finishing his cake. "It's all a question of timing, Tilt. You're right, if the plays were good once then they're good still" - I almost interrupt on the use of the word 'if' - "but it only takes one rotten apple - one *perceived* rotten apple - to spoil the barrel."

I allow him his correction from some rudimentary sense of sympathy, probably misplaced; publisher or not, words are not really Justin's thing. There is no way *Rust* is a 'rotten apple'.

"So what you're saying is…"

"That we put the project on hold. Just for a while. Until your next play -"

"Your next triumph," Duncan suggests.

"Indeed. Triumph." Justin picks up on the word. "And then we go again. Just as we planned."

"No more than a rain-check," Duncan offers, inserting himself back into the fray.

Aware that I have been ganged-up on, caught in a pincer movement, I look down at the table and see three empty cups and two empty plates. I realise there is something significant there, a metaphor you could actually do something with - but now's not the time to pull out the notebook from my silk-lined pocket.

"But what do *you* think? Both of you?"

"Think?"

I smile to myself as Justin proves a point.

"About what?"

"About *Rust*, Duncan." I lean in to emphasise intensity, importance. "If we ignore the Adelphi and the so-called reviews for just for a moment, what do you think about my 'rotten apple'." Okay, so I was unable to let it go after all. Justin shows signs that he is about to bluster and protest. "Have you seen it? Have you read it?" I ensure I include Justin in the second question.

"I was at some of the rehearsals, of course." Duncan colours. "And I'd planned to go to the premier, but it you remember Mandy wasn't well…" He allows his excuse to trail away.

"And what did you think?"

"About the play?"

"No, Duncan, about the architecture! Of course about the fucking play!" Low blow or not, it does nothing to reduce the colour in his cheeks. He glances up from the table and into the general throng, almost as it he is hoping someone will come riding to his rescue.

"I think you have a point about the guy playing Rodri."

He needs say nothing more. My agent hasn't even bothered to see the damn play, so how can I expect him to adequately defend me? I turn to Justin.

"And you?"

"I confess I haven't seen it, Tilt. I'm not really a theatre kind of man."

I wonder what kind of man he is, exactly.

"But you've read it. I mean, you were going to publish the thing, after all."

His slight pause gives me my answer before he does.

"One of my team - Kasey - she's read it. She's the one working on your book, so it made sense. Obviously."

"And what did she think? Or don't you know?"

It is, I realise, a moment of high drama. If we were on the stage at this precise instant (and in a way we are, of course), then the audience would be expecting something to happen. It would be my responsibility - my characters' responsibility - to make something happen. I glance to Duncan, back to Justin, and then to Duncan again.

Timing being everything, I wait just long enough and then stand.

"Gentlemen, we are finished for today I think. You know how to get hold of me."

Bereft of handshakes, my sudden retreat is met with silence - evidence of the effectiveness of the little scene I have just created. I walk away half-prepared to hear Duncan trying to call me back - though what I'll do if he does is a next step I haven't had time to consider. I pass the waitress who served us and smile beatifically, hoping it's a gesture sufficient to pass on the message that my premature departure has nothing to do with her. Although she nods in recognition, I instantly get the impression that I am just another face, another punter. Are she and I alike in that regard; operating in an insular world where those around us are - at least on a daily basis - largely insignificant? After all, how would it be possible for everyone to be of fundamental importance to everyone else? And Duncan and Justin: how significant are they?

It is a question I take with me through the atrium, past the shop, past the security guards (who, perhaps oddly, pay no attention to those leaving the building), and out into the explosion that is London. There are echoes of my emergence from King's Cross, not only in the sudden intrusion of noise, but also because of a certain frisson in the air. All around me there is dynamism. Things are happening, moving on - yet apparently *Rust* is no longer one of those things. Without thinking, I find myself standing at the pop-up café and ordering another Americano, hoping this one will be hot. For no real reason other than corporate process - especially given

I am the only one in the queue at this precise moment - the barista asks my name. I know she is going to write it on the faux cardboard cup with which I will eventually be presented, and that she will announce its availability to the world using my name: "Americano for Tilt!" For an instant I shy away from the prospect. "Rodri" I tell her, using the first name that comes into my head. I wonder if the choice is ironic.

Once united with my coffee, I find a vacant table on the perimeter of the café's allotted space and sit in one of its accompanying metal-mesh chairs, choosing the best view of the entrance to the BL. I'm not sure if I feel like a guard or a spy, but know I have chosen the spot in order to look out for Duncan or Justin leaving the building. And if Duncan should do so first, will I be tempted to call him over, even apologise for my outburst? I don't see why I should; it would be a little like an organ grinder apologising to his monkey. In fact I wonder if it shouldn't be the opposite, he apologising to me. Or perhaps I ought to have fought my corner with a little more vigour; a threat wouldn't have been out of the question. "And that next play, my next 'triumph'," I might have said, "perhaps I should take it elsewhere…" Undoubtedly a cheap shot and probably not one befitting a sophisticated playwright such as the Great Tilt - but on the other hand, why not? There are stories - some of them legendary - about such encounters and their outcomes. And Duncan is exactly the kind of man likely to succumb to the tactic; wasn't he so recently nervous about the prospects for our conversation? What did that say about him? I don't doubt as they sat there in the wake of my withdrawal that they would have spoken about me, compared notes, asked each other what they should do next. It's easier for Justin, of course; he simply has to wait. He - or Kelsey, to be precise - has already made the effort, the bulk of the work is done. Timing; that's all he needs to worry about. Which is probably just as well for someone with a stain on the lapel of their suit. But Duncan; what does he want?

As I weigh-up the question, I watch the comings and goings of people across the concourse: little groups of Japanese tourists in uniform beige macs; people who have business - *serious* business from their perspective - within the library; those who have found their way here by mistake, wandering in from Euston Road expecting to find a museum or art gallery. And here and there, still a punctuation of the young, the students, the bare-middled girls who are presumably grateful that it appears to be getting a little warmer.

Duncan, I decide, wants an easy life. He can do without the kind of stress *Rust* is currently putting on him and which I have just exacerbated. Well, serves him right. He would probably like me to revert to type; to go back to producing material that was easy to sell to theatres. The Adelphi, he might argue, took *Rust* on the strength of my earlier work rather than on the strength of the play itself. Whether he has a point or not, it is a game I have no inclination to play. 'Traditional Tilt' is what he wants. And I suspect he doesn't actually want a triumph, but rather a 'hit'. There's a subtle difference. 'Hits' make more money. Perhaps years ago I might have crumbled, caved in. Before I was a name - and all the while I longed to become one - I would have been prepared to engage on his terms. I take the lid from my coffee cup and place it on the table, watching the steam rise. "Be honest Tilt, that was a game you *did* play!" I can't help but smile to myself.

Taking a sip of the hot liquid, over the rim of the cup I notice Justin leaving the building. Without any kind of pause, rather than cross the concourse he heads left and takes the more direct through to St Pancras. I watch him walk. His gait is commercial rather than artistic; he has the air of a man who surrounds himself with the material and tangible, and likes to think he has a nose for the finer things in life. Again the equation of Justin-equals-books fails to resolve itself. Where Duncan wants to settle for an easy life, Justin demands of himself nothing less than adherence to the pecuniary. What was it he said: "put your project on hold until the next play…" Next play what? Makes money, I assume. Which would make both their lives easier of course.

Then a question drags me back into our temporary triumvirate: "And what about you, Tilt, Old Boy? What do you want?" Or is it easier to say what I don't want? I have - in common parlance - established a lifestyle to which I have become accustomed. And I don't simply mean money; I would argue it's about more than something which can be defined so lazily or be so self-evidently superficial. Through my work - whether consciously or not, who knows? - I have built foundations upon which I can now construct a castle, the impressive edifice for which Tilt will truly be remembered. And *Rust* was supposed to be the first segment of battlements, or the first tower, rising above everything I have done before. No. It *is* the first component. "I have nothing to declare…" But Duncan wants me to go back to digging ditches and putting in more foundations just for the sake of it - and presumably because it pays. Maybe he doesn't see me as a castle builder - but how the hell would he know, he hasn't even seen the play! So unlike my two erstwhile companions, where they desire another 'hit', perhaps I crave a 'triumph' of a different kind - and one in the truer sense of the word.

Once, very early on in our association, Duncan remarked that, in spite of what everyone thought, mine was actually a very crowded field. "Oh, people focus on the big names, of course they do," he said, "and then in consequence draw the erroneous conclusion that there are actually very few playwrights. But there are thousands." Still wet behind the ears at that point, I asked him what he meant. "Stick to what you're good at, at what earns you a living. Then you'll be fine. But don't get ideas above your station." Did I follow his recommendation slavishly? Not entirely. If I had there would be no Tilt as we know and love him today, no book deal with Justin, no run - however short! - at the Adelphi. No *Rust*. Perhaps that's what he and Justin talked about when I left. Maybe Duncan leant across the table and, in what he might have imagined as a conspiratorial voice, pointed out "I knew this would happen; I told him what to do and what to stick to." Well, I've proved him wrong before and I'll do so again. Others may be happy to 'dumb down' and stick in their little niche, but I don't see why I should - especially when I've got more to offer. Head above the parapet stuff, that's what we're talking about. Better; building the parapet first!

This 'staying in your comfort zone' is a drum I've heard Justin beat too. He loves to trot out examples from the world of fiction, authors who are solid and reliable, churn out the same thing over and over again because the people love it: same plot, just change the names of the characters. You know who they are. Isn't that just a little fraudulent, taking punters for a ride? Or is it the punters' fault? He told me how much he thinks some of them earn - not that I'll ever be in that kind of bracket, I accept that. When he did so I couldn't help but imagine him drooling and wishing I was one such author. Who the hell made money out of publishing a book of plays?

Which is why I'm guessing he delegated the job to Kelsey. Well, fuck him then. Mine isn't the persona of someone who's content to just turn the handle is it? I mean, I ask you!

Having said all of that, I confess I *have* tried to write fiction more than once. I glance across to the entrance to the building and watch people come and go, try an imagine their lives, the narratives in which I could place them. There are stories that could be built, contexts drawn, defined and refined; webs to be woven across dozens and dozens of pages and tens of thousands of words… If thus far I've tried and failed, do I truly know that I can't do it? It's only when my characters speak they come alive; everything else has run the risk of being just cliché, cardboard scenery, hackneyed bollocks. For a very brief time I had this notion of one day turning in a thousand pages of prose to Duncan, elegant and fluent prose which blew his socks off. Instantaneously I would be transformed from playwright to best-selling author; a prodigy of some kind. Well I haven't done so thus far, of course. Maybe some of that coincidentally justifies his "stick to what you know" mantra - but only at the micro level. At the macro, I want to move on. *Rust* was moving on. *Rust* was proving I could do more. *Rust* is the future.

"Is it?"

Not only is the question unexpected, I would not have imagined me being the one to ask it. I look around where I'm sitting to check that Duncan hasn't managed to escape the BL without me seeing him; that he hasn't crept up behind me to whisper in my ear. It is, after all, precisely the question I assume he wanted to ask - but lacked the courage to do so. But not only is he nowhere to be seen, the voice in which the question has been asked is undoubtedly my own; an echo from "And what do you want?"

I shiver involuntarily and glance down to where my coffee cup now stands empty. I don't recall the moment I finished drinking. Perhaps it was lost amid my ruminations about writing fiction. Obviously there is nothing of consequence in finishing my drink - at least not in comparison with hearing the words "Is it?" accost me. As little more than a diversionary tactic, I check my watch. Nearly twelve. The time throws me, both in its passing and its tardiness. I had assumed that the meeting with Duncan - and only Duncan! - would follow the normal format of our jovial, innocent get togethers; that one coffee would extend to two, and then coffee would turn into lunch. We had form at the BL, and their lunch offerings were usually entirely passable. On that basis - National Portrait Gallery notwithstanding - I had not expected to emerge until nearly two, at which point a stroll back to the station and a quick drink would have rounded off the day. But now? Not only has that not happened, I find myself outside, alone, and with time to kill. Given I had met Duncan a little before eleven, why was it still only twelve? Looking towards Euston Road - perhaps hoping to find an answer somewhere between here and there - the voice asks again "Is it?"

I wonder if the question might now refer to the time, as if I have managed to simultaneously externalise and vocalise my doubt about the hour. And yet I suspect this other voice is still hung-up on *Rust* and beginning to fixate on the whole ditch-digger versus wall-builder debate. I try an internal smile; sit a little more upright; glance at the lining of my jacket; admit to the shine on my shoes; think back to those unfortunates with whom I shared the railway carriage on the way into town. All the usual tricks. "Tilt, Old Boy…" I begin - and then find that there is nothing following on.

12:00

Toby shakes his head and moves again, setting off on a loop around the periphery of the small lake. He is immediately struck by the difference in the shape and scale of it depending on where you are, and it occurs to him that appreciation of life is a little like that, influenced by your status in relation to it, what your viewpoint is. Surely his own perspective has been corrupted by the accident and its outcome? Isn't his issue not where he is on his journey, but how he chooses to look forward? If that is so, he feels perfectly entitled to dismiss out-of-hand the argument that he is damaged goods and no better than average. All that nonsense about prosecution and defence! He pauses at the end of the lake near a signpost promising a restaurant nearby and checks his watch. Just after twelve.

As he heads towards his lunch stop - the awnings of the café visible ahead of him - a shout from his right catches his attention. Where the park opens out into a broader expanse, a group of people are playing rounders. Evidently the batter has just sent the ball toward what would, in cricketing terms, be 'long on', and is now haring round the bases as two of the opposition chase down his blow. Given the fundamentals of hand-eye coordination are the same as cricket, he is certain he would be good at rounders. Yet it is not a game for which he has ever had much time - though having said that, what wouldn't he give to be able to cast his crutch aside and join in? It is a pang of regret which merely serves to reinforce what he already knows: not only how much he loves cricket, but how important it is to him. Toby momentarily visualises the sport as a being little like the aluminium stick on which he currently relies, a support which helps him keep him in balance. He smiles somewhat wistfully at this further excursion into philosophy, though this time strives to chase it away in a positive fashion. Hasn't he been lucky to have been able to play for as long as he has, and at a decent standard too? Doesn't he have a few more years left yet, even if there are youngsters who will soon get the better of him? On that basis there are things to be anticipated, namely that first training session next year, his first match back? If he were to be here in twelve months time, why wouldn't he be able to join and make a good fist of it? Resolved to this upbeat view he arrives at the café, finds a free table and scans the menu.

Three minutes later a member of the waiting staff, dressed in the establishment's two-tone green uniform, arrives at his table. Expecting to see him in black and white - doesn't every server in the country wear black and white? - Toby is momentarily thrown, unsure whether he approves. Presumably the outfit is designed to give a nod to the location.

"What can I get you?"

The waiter pulls what looks like an iPhone from his apron pocket and stands poised, gadget in one hand, thin stylus in the other. As Toby orders, each item is accompanied by a tap of the stylus on the device; then the waiter repeats what is on his screen.

"Is that correct?" he asks.

"Thank you."

There is another tap and the waiter turns.

"Is that it?" Toby asks, holding the young man there.

"I'm sorry?"

"Don't you have to write something down? If not now, when you get back to the kitchen."

The waiter smiles.

"No, sir. As soon as I confirmed your order - that last tap - it appeared on a screen in the kitchen." He wafts the phone in Toby's general direction. "By the time I get back there they will already be working on it. In fact, I suspect your coffee is being prepared as we speak."

There is something of the triumphant in the way the explanation is delivered.

"That sounds remarkably efficient," Toby concedes.

"It is." The young man smiles. "Means my life is so much easier. It's almost impossible to make a mistake, so we get happy customers - and *you* get served just that little bit quicker." He pauses for a moment, then nods, replaces the device in his pocket and heads back toward the main building.

The exchange prompts Toby to remember the software 'task force' at work. Thus far everyone involved has been vaguely uncertain as to the project's exact remit and what its end-goals might be. Without explicitly wishing to, he cannot help but draw a parallel between what he does professionally and the processes followed by the waiter - both previous and current. Might new software not work the same for him? Click, click, easy-peasy. No-mistake calculations delivered more quickly, without nuance, interpretation - and without the input of years of experience. Is that where the task force is heading? It is not difficult for him to understand why they might wish to do so; commoditisation is the modern-day mantra, so why should his profession be any different? However, restaurants still need waiters to take orders - to put stylus to screen - and then deliver food to the tables. Technology hadn't come that far, not yet anyway. But in his case? Not only is there a general decline in demand for annuity-related products and services, people increasingly expect to execute transactions more quickly than ever; more often than not they will do so on-line and assume they'll be served by a slick interface and only need human intervention when there is a problem. Was that what he was destined to become, a kind of financial troubleshooter? Having already had the discussion with himself about his problem-solving abilities, might he actually be staring into something far worse? Might they cease to need him at all? It is not too large a leap to make, a scenario entirely within the realms of possibility. And then what? He was forty-six; for over twenty years he had been in the same game, crunching the same numbers, coming up with subtle variations, smuggling profits into - and then out of - premiums. What else could he do if the need to keep on doing that was taken away from him?

Just at that moment the waiter returns with his coffee, panini, and cake, lifting them from a tray and placing the three items on the table in front of him.

"There," he says, still with that triumphant air, "just like I said."

He pauses for a moment, expecting acknowledgement - but all Toby can do is stare at his lunch as if it has just betrayed him.

Whether the food is bland and tasteless is debatable, but it seems exactly so to Toby at that moment. Working his way through the panini with little enthusiasm, as a distraction he scans patrons sitting at the other tables, trying to summon up sufficient interest in them to see if he can divine at least a part of their stories. But all he succeeds in doing is to wonder what they might see if *they* looked *his* way: a man who arrived at the café a few minutes earlier with a brightening mood, focussed on the most promising elements of his future life and determined to cling to those? If so, they may have also seen his determination proven to be fragile, blown to smithereens by a young man armed with nothing more than a phone; a device which has suddenly come to act as a metaphor for something that may be an existential threat to that very same future. Given the ups and downs of the emotional rollercoaster on which he currently seems trapped, he can only ask whether that bleaker outlook for his work is a valid scenario. And even if it is, what has new technology got to do with playing cricket again, the thrill of taking a wicket or the blissful experience of watching a late cut race to the boundary?

A family of four arrives at a table on the far side of the café: a couple and their two children. The legendary nuclear family. Just like he and Marita, Alex and Lucinda. What has work's project to do with them? On the face of it, nothing at all. Yet it is the findings of the task force Toby fears most; the unknown. Not because they will shake the foundations of what he has built up over time - his own nuclear family - but because of the collateral damage caused by a potential reduction in income, loss of self-esteem. Who knows where that might lead?

As a unit he assumes they are strong enough to survive. Hasn't he built-up sufficient financial reserves over the years to provide a buffer against what would surely prove merely temporary hardship? Their collective life has conformed to all expected norms of love, education, support; they have taken their fair share of holidays, enjoyed an appropriate level of fun. Toby imagines himself flicking through the family photographs stored on his laptop and is confident he could conjure the story relating to each of them: how Alex had fallen in Windermere that time after standing up in their rowing boat; how Lucinda had been knocked into a cowpat having turned her back on a particularly frisky goat. There were images from sports days and school plays, from trips to museums. Toby expected he would even be able to find happy images from that dreadful trip to the National History Museum! Wasn't all that worth something alongside the drawings and paintings the kids had made before they could draw and paint properly - and which Marita had judiciously kept? If he needed to compile evidence to prove the security of his family unit, surely he could find it in abundance.

On the far table there is a burst of laughter and photographs being taken, a joke shared. The father is making a show of looking shocked or distraught or upset. Such things resonated too; if he looked hard enough (and possibly not even that hard) couldn't Toby polish the mirrors held up by other people and see reflected in them how rich and fulfilling his own family life had been? Can be still. Or be again. Surely.

But what of Marita? She is suddenly front and centre in his memory. Toby remembers the 'Go Ape' experience she absolutely hated and how grumpy she had been for ages afterwards - something which only served to make the children's excitement even more of an annoyance to her; annoyance captured in fragmentary images. But there is a difference between the remembered and the digital Marita. Over the last few years she has been in fewer of the photographs, often because she was taking the picture; and when she does appear, the children remain the centre of attention, their mother an appendage. Toby wonders if any of that actually matters; whether such things are examples which serve to demonstrate how she has been successfully fulfilling her destiny, an ambition for life laid out for her by her mother and her mother's mother before her. Theirs is a well-ingrained Eastern European tradition, a path so well-trodden that perhaps it has ceased to be a path and become a rut. Yet did that bother Marita? Had she even recognised it? Moreover, had he? Perhaps that was the larger question. Toby watches the other mother pick up her phone again to take another photo, this time of one of the children staring off into the mid-distance, their attention grabbed by something external to the family group. And the father, in that moment, looking *her* way. What is *he* thinking? Is there a growing distance there too, one germinated by age, watered by tiredness and preoccupation?

For a moment Toby feels the pang of loss as if he has dropped something along the way, like keys inadvertently falling from a pocket. Or that yard of pace on the cricket pitch. Knowing he will never get the latter back, he forces himself to ask about Marita; has he lost something in relation to her too? It is inevitable they are not the people they once were? They had been young and idealistic, crashing into each other at a mutual friend's birthday party and becoming instantly inseparable. They will never experience that frisson again - nor its passion, lust, love. Such loss is, he tells himself, unavoidable; and he tells himself he is reconciled to that fact, just as he assumes Marita must be. Indeed, as all the evidence suggests. But that does not exempt him from remembering those days - those feelings - with a sense of longing. Just as he wishes he could bowl again as he did against Old Cuthbertians, so he imagines dusting off experiences from his early days with Marita and reliving them. Surely that would make everything right - even to the extent of completely dissolving the threat from the task force, or the youngsters coming through from the junior team. But even as he tries to persuade himself of this - in spite of its impossibility! - he knows there is another strand to the story.

Finding himself transported back to Bolsover once more, he looks around with some urgency, trying to locate a waiter who might rescue him by presenting the bill. He has no desire to revisit Derbyshire again. Going through the process of paying, standing up, walking away, would surely anchor him in the present. But there is no-one suitable within view, and even though he tries to focus on how his Achilles is feeling, the distraction is too weak not to see Toby suddenly returned to Bolsover castle.

She had pressed against him thanks to a slip on a step, his hand out instinctively to catch her. In itself, it had been an insignificant incident, yet it had given her permission to penetrate the space around him, a space she was only too happy to occupy. Claiming a desire to visit a relative living nearby, she had begged they take her car; yet when they left the castle she asked him to drive, selecting a minor route back to the hotel where, presumably, the others had most likely already given up on their game of cards. Toby had been concentrating on navigating a particularly narrow stretch of road when he felt her hand on his thigh. Having to focus on his driving, he had been unable to prevent her hand travelling quickly to his groin, feeling for his penis through the cotton of his chinos. Not wishing to replay this memory any further, he half stands, looking again for a server to come to his aid - but he is as powerless now as he had been then. By the time she had unzipped his trousers, she had directed him to a track which turned away from the road before petering out at a rusted five-bar gate. Opening her door, she had ordered him into the back of car. As soon as he had complied she had loosed his belt and helped him lower his trousers. His penis stood erect in her hand. Moments later, she had straddled him and with a magician's sleight of hand, slipped it inside her. Toby wants to recall a shout, a protest, but all that comes back to him is the thrill of it, the danger, the excitement, as if she had given him the chance to rediscover something too long lost. As she rode him she had whispered "not yet, not yet", but no matter how hard he tried he had been unable to restrain himself for very long, grabbing her waist and pulling her hard onto him as he came. In a few seconds he was spent. But the climax had not been a mutual one. Taking his right hand, she placed his fingers on her clitoris and, with him still inside her, said "now my turn; finish me off". And he had done so, just as Marita had taught him all those years before.

But this had not been Marita.

"Have you finished, sir?" The voice of a waiter rouses him from his past. "Was everything satisfactory?"

For a moment Toby is unsure how to answer the question. Had it been satisfactory? Any of it?

"Yes. Thank you."

A phone and stylus is produced from an apron pocket once again and, after two swift taps, the screen is then consulted. The server informs Toby how much he owes, then produces another device - this one white and like a small box - which he holds out. Opening his wallet, Toby selects a card and presses it against the waiting gadget, their union sealed with a perfunctory beep.

Noticing the table which had hosted the family is now vacant, he stands and begins to walk away. After a few strides his progress is halted by the waiter who, in clearing the table, has rescued the crutch Toby had inadvertently left behind. Were he in the right frame of mind to do so, he might have chosen to ask whether his forgetting it was an early indication that he didn't really need it. But once again he is in no mood to be positive.

~

"Imogen."

She turns. A man - mid-forties, nice suit, no tie - is walking into the room, extending his hand.

"Alastair," she says confidently.

"Anthony, actually." He laughs. "Alistair's just behind me, getting a coffee." She tries not to blush. Anthony indicates the place where her handbag rests on the table. "Please, sit down."

Imogen sets her half-empty glass on the table, her bag on the floor beside her chair, and sits. As soon as she does so, Alastair enters the room and places his coffee on the table, choosing the seat nearest the door. With him sitting between Anthony and Imogen, they will occupy three sides of the table - unconventional for an interview. Alastair is taller, older, wearing a tie; and although he is smiling too, Imogen detects a certain edge about him.

"Alastair Burgess," the new man offers.

Briefly standing to shake his hand, she assumes he is the senior of the two.

"Thank you for coming to see us Imogen," Anthony says, taking the lead. "We'll take about fifty minutes or so I expect. Usual interview format; no trick questions, that's not our style!" It is an offer to laugh, an attempt to put her at her ease. Imogen recognises it as such and responds appropriately. "My name's Anthony Griffiths; I'm one of the HR managers here. I'm sure Alastair will elaborate later on, but for now all you need to know is that he runs one of the three divisions we have here, and that it's for a position in his division we're recruiting."

Imogen nods.

"Perhaps," Alastair interjects, his voice strangely monotone and immediately giving the impression he has done this kind of thing far too often for his liking, "we could start with you telling us what the agent has told you about the position for which you've applied, and what you know of our company. After that we'll walk through your cv and see where that takes us."

From page one of the interview manual; a textbook opening. Imogen thinks of the notes she made in the little book buried in her handbag. She smiles briefly, ensures she is sitting bolt upright, then responds.

＊

"I'm interested in hearing about the specific deliverables for which you've had responsibility."

Half-an-hour in and they have been through her cv. Largely it has been Imogen speaking, prompted by both Alastair and Anthony. Not quite 'good-cop, bad-cop', Anthony has been interested in the emotional and organisational side of her professional journey, Alastair on the practical. She feels she has handled them both well, demonstrated efficiency and fluency, kept them on track. Wanting to be as much in control of the process as possible, she has even disagreed with them once or twice to demonstrate she knows what she is talking about. Why would they want to hire someone who didn't? Or someone who is weak? Alastair's latest request - delivered as he pushes her cv slightly away from him and eases himself back into his chair - has surprised her.

"Deliverables?" Her question - and the uncertainty it fails to mask - is out before she can stop it.

"Yes. I don't mean the standard PA-type activities we've already talked about. If we didn't think you could arrange meetings or travel, take notes, write emails etcetera - well, you wouldn't be here." She smiles, trying to show appreciation. Alastair glances at his colleague.

"Of course." Anthony backs him up. "But these days an EA is much more of a rounded person, don't you think? And especially in our business. For example, not just arranging a conference but potentially acting as host, or even speaking at it. It's clear that you have the discipline and application needed to fulfil standard tasks given you, but your cv most definitely suggests there are other things - shall we call them 'projects' - which you have taken on yourself. If not actually initiated. That's what we're interested to hear about."

Imogen feels herself redden slightly. She glances to the window and where London suddenly seems to be receding further into the distance as if it were a dolly-shot in a Hitchcock movie. Was that *Vertigo*? Back on the table, her cv stares up at her, its words blurring momentarily. If she had been guilty of anything in its construction she might admit to a little 'gilding-the-lily'. Her first draft had been bland; 'standard' to use Anthony's word. It had read too much like that of a modest PA. Not only was that not how she saw herself, more importantly it was not the role she was chasing.

Being an EA in The Shard said so much more about who she wanted to be! And so in places she had implied that some of the things she had achieved were more important than they actually were, or suggested she had a hand in the shaping of things and taken original ideas to Sonia which had been accepted and then acted upon. If most of this was only tangentially true, the important end result was a cv capable of impressing; it had got her through the filtering process, the front doors, up in the lift. Yet it represented a version of her still cloaked in aspiration. It was the cv she wanted to be able to write *after* she had worked in London - in The Shard - for three years. Was it such a crime to want to try and tilt things in her favour?

Hardly in a position to back-track, Imogen chooses to go on the offensive. She returns to some of the things about which she has already spoken and reframes them in slightly different language, as if verbalising the gilding she had applied to the paper: she offers some criticism of Sonia, suggesting where she had needed to compensate for her boss's shortcomings; she inflates her standing a little, changes her tone - and before she knows it, finds herself playing the role of Sonia herself. Once she has inadvertently landed on this stratagem, second-hand familiarity allows her answers flow with more authority. She watches Alastair nod once or twice, glance toward Anthony. When they seek clarification, Imogen frames her response by trying to recall what Sonia did or would have done, tweaking it accordingly. And in a way, why not? Doesn't she want to show them she meets the specification of the person they seek? Aren't they actually looking for someone like Sonia, someone who could 'be' Sonia? And why can't that be her?

Fifteen minutes later she is standing with Anthony in reception waiting for a lift to take her back to ground level.

"You were actually the last person we were planning to see," he says, glancing away from her to the illuminated numbers above one of the sets of doors as it counts down to seventeen, "and given that - and also that we're always pretty prompt when it comes to interview responses - you should hear back from the agency today. It seems only fair; not to draw things out, I mean."

"Of course," she smiles, trying to appear confident, knowing. "I'll look forward to the feedback."

Whether or not Anthony intended to respond he offers nothing else, his attention diverted by a lift's arrival and its doors opening. He takes a step towards it and holds out his hand. Closure.

"And thank you again for coming."

And then Imogen is in the lift, turning just before the door closes to see Anthony walking towards the reception desk, mid-way through a gesture she is unable to translate.

~

Lawrence wonders if that was largely how their meeting had been, 'inconclusive'. It is an observation reached too quickly, almost as soon as he sets off towards Waterloo Bridge, and one which, once it has possessed him, he feels the need to challenge. Inevitably it is easier to start with Tessa. At least she had tried. Lawrence feels the residual sensation of her hand on his arm, the remnants of that hug. The evidence of a more collaborative past was buried there somewhere, an echo of a time when they had been on the same side - though against whom he is unsure. Most often it would have been Dylan. The echo leads him to wonder about his siblings' modern-day relationship; did it remain as unbalanced as it had always been? Yet she had made an effort, called him 'Larry', asked the more significant questions. It wasn't exactly a fresh start, though; more like someone returning a long-overdue book to the library - and perhaps a book for which he had been searching. Yet even so, in Tessa's case Lawrence almost found his self-concern trumped by his worry for her. He hadn't expected her to look so changed, and the news about Penny had surprised him even more. As he walks past a few skateboarders turning tricks in a concrete canyon, he can't help but recognise her as the closest he now has to a kindred spirit; after all, they have both lost someone in addition to their mother. She had suggested he try to pray again, and he wonders whether her advice came from personal experience - not that there is any evidence of spiritual dialogue on her side. Or of nothing which had been successful.

Emerging from beneath Waterloo Bridge, the National Theatre rises to his right and people drift in and out through its many entrances. He imagines them buying tickets or souvenirs, or having coffee. The latter is something he might have been tempted to do had he not just finished his second latte - for which Dylan had paid and for which Lawrence tries to give him due credit, even though, under the circumstances, he really didn't have any alternative. Firstly he is the eldest and probably the most solvent, and secondly he was highly unlikely to have risked creating a scene in front of Tessa by insisting his baby brother pay. "Your idea, you cough up." Lawrence tries a small inward smile to see if free coffee feels like a triumph, however minor. Perhaps calling him 'Larry' was always going to be a step too far for Dylan, but there may have been (if he searches hard enough) the odd glimmer of hope, of fellow-feeling. It is at this point - just as he beings to approach the old 'OXO' building - that Lawrence realises he simply doesn't care. As he glances up, the letters on the building's tower - that iconic 'O', 'X', 'O' combination - suddenly remind him of fruitless games of noughts-and-crosses played with his brother when he was a child. When Dylan went first he never lost, always ruthlessly capitalising on any mistake an infant Lawrence made; and when *he* went first, a draw was the best he could hope for. It had been a mental duel Dylan used to torture him for a year or two, a simple way to demonstrate superiority - at least until Lawrence's growing maturity and understanding forced the game into perpetual stalemate. Yet he *had* cared desperately how the game turned out, and remembers occasions when persistent defeat sent him crying to his mother. But as he sees the letters now, prominent and - of course! - inconclusive too, he feels as if he can finally let them and their childhood game go. They are no longer relevant; nor is that part of his past relevant. And Dylan? Is he now irrelevant? Lawrence thinks of Tessa and begins to draft out a simple sum in imaginary pencil in his mind; it sits above two parallel lines beneath which an answer is expected. If it represents part of the overall equation he is trying to solve, Lawrence wonders if his current internal debate is no more than him working things out in the margin.

Keen to leave the OXO building behind him, he follows the Thames Path as it skirts a large office complex, a residential block, and then ducks under Blackfriars' road and rail bridges. As the vista opens out, Lawrence moderates his pace slightly. For no good reason he can think of he had started to walk a little quicker and, checking his watch, reaffirms he has time on his side. There is no need to rush. And what has he to rush for anyway, other than the arbitrarily chosen 3 p.m. train from King's Cross? Tessa and Dylan will have separated, Tessa presumably back to her now unshared flat near the Oval, and Dylan… Lawrence realises he has no idea where Dylan currently lives. He recalls that he and Sarah had initially set-up together in Kensal Rise, and then moved elsewhere as promotions and salaries permitted them to do so. Children must have forced at least one subsequent move, but to where Lawrence is unsure. Part of him wants to locate Dylan somewhere beginning with 'B': Bermondsey, Bexhill, Ealing Broadway, Barking? And for the second time in quick succession he tells himself he doesn't care about that either, realisations which strike him like the tolling of a bell.

As soon as he is parallel with the Tate, Lawrence walks to the edge of the path, leans against the wall, and looks out over the water. To his right people traverse the Millennium Bridge, while across the river the dome of St Paul's rises above the rooftops. Is that a sign of some kind? For a moment he wonders if he should heed Tessa's advice and seek a little silent contemplation; to see if he is able to rekindle enough of his belief to allow God back in; to find out if a new prayer is all it would take. But tempting though the notion is, he knows St Pauls is not the place; how could he expect peace and quiet in a tourist attraction? An image of money-lenders in the temple comes to him, and so he turns his back on the scene to examine the right-angled solidity of the ex-power station. God and art: two different passions in two different architectures. Not that he has ever had any interest in art. When he left home he tried to generate an enthusiasm for it, telling himself that a broader appreciation would enhance his role as librarian. But, in spite of his love of books and literature, liberal art as manifested in paintings and sculpture left him cold. He believes he is able to appreciate something when it is well executed - a Leonardo painting or Michelangelo figure - but the ability to understand hidden meaning is a challenge on a different plain entirely. Looking at the Tate - and almost attempting to see through its solid walls and into the exhibitions housed there - he wonders how much of this lack of connection is down to failure of imagination and how much upbringing; after all, Dylan and Tessa were never particularly artistic either. "Nature versus nurture?" he mentally offers to the world in general, not expecting an answer. Perhaps a few months ago, when he was still believing, a voice might have whispered the answer. In its absence he suspects the answer is 'both'.

As he resumes his walk he sees an elderly woman coming towards him. She is clearly frail and uses a stick for support, but there is about her - in the way she looks ahead, the way she is dressed - an undeniable air of independence. Passing her, their eyes meet for the briefest of moments before he looks away, yet it is enough for him to steal her physicality and house his mother within it, imagining how she might have looked had she survived and then come to London, perhaps to visit Tessa or Dylan. He sees her announcing that she will go for a little walk, that she does not need any assistance - nor anyone to go with her! - and imagines himself watching as she sets off for the tube, perhaps at Barking or Ealing Broadway or some such. Not only does he suddenly feel as if he has been robbed, but he realises he has caught in the old woman's eye a glint of accusation, her awareness of what he did two years previously and why he looked at her in the way he just has. Expecting immediate condemnation from over his shoulder, he scans the scene about him fearing everyone will now be looking his way, pointing at the man who betrayed his mother. And even though no-one does - indeed, all those he can see care even less about him than he does about Dylan - he feels crushed once again. The old question of abandonment resurrects itself and he strives to bat it away, just as he has been doing for these past few months. He explained what happened to Dylan and Tessa just now, didn't he? And surely *he* believed what he'd said? Wanting to hear God's voice, that reassurance, he looks up just as he reaches an slightly uneven section of paving. His stumble (the inevitable consequence) is no more than a stutter, but he feels it magnified many times over, and so he stops to regather himself and looks again over his shoulder. Still no-one is interested in him, and the old woman with the stick is no longer visible, absorbed into the day. The idea that she was never there at all - but rather a chimera or a messenger from on high - flashes through his mind then dissipates as if it were no more than a brief cloud of cigarette smoke. Lawrence looks out to the river once more, to where that smoke might have drifted, hoping to find reassurance in the Thames's reliability - and finds himself suddenly wishing he were not in London at all.

But there is no smoke, and to those without a photographic memory the Thames appears as it did five, ten, thirty minutes ago. Or two years ago. It is as if the landscape is scrolling alongside a stationary and unchanging river, Lawrence being carried along with it, his perambulation an illusion. Ahead and to his right Shakespeare's 'Globe' returns him to more familiar territory, easing him away from the impenetrability of art and into the concrete of text. The link is comforting; for Lawrence it feels like being thrown a lifebelt having strayed out of his depth. Books. The library. Not that he pretends to understand the Bard; rather, it is the milieu which offers comfort. Still wrestling with the experience of his earlier meeting, the appearance of the old woman, the nagging of his history, the absence of God, he suddenly wants to find a parallel in the plays. A translation of reality, an alternate perspective would be welcome. Someone once told him that Shakespeare's work offered answers to any question if only you took the trouble to look. He approaches a noticeboard advertising the season's programme hopeful that, even based on his limited knowledge, he might find a clue, a key to help him unravel what increasingly feels like a puzzle for which he has no picture.

The current production - *King Lear* - strikes him as unlikely territory in which to find a template he could use to decode his situation. There are three siblings in *Lear*, but beyond that? Not that he, Dylan and Tessa have much in common with Lear's daughters, and if he were inclined to eschew convention and cast himself in the role of the wronged Cordelia, that would mean Dylan and Tessa would have to take on Gonerill and Regan. Hardly fair, at least not on Tessa. Lawrence rakes through the embers of his memory. Weren't there also brothers in the story? Scanning the poster he finds references to Edmund and Edgar. He knows one was good and one evil but, unable to recall which was which, cannot cast those parts either. And his mother? Or his father, come to that? Finding the future schedule, he scans for something more suitable. *Hamlet*, perhaps - at least there is a mother and father there. Or one of the comedies? If he wishes to be flooded with insight he is disappointed; it seems Shakespeare is unlikely to speak to him - at least not in the way God would have. Again Lawrence misses the insight of that voice, the comfort blanket it offered. Against such a measure, what is Shakespeare, he asks himself; no more than a minstrel? And if that is the case, no matter how exceptional a minstrel he may be, what does that say about everyone else, all those others who have put words together, bound them between covers, the very bricks of his library? Or what of his own existence in that vast context? How can he possibly question that? Wanting to find solutions, the last thing he needs is more uncertainty. Moving briskly away from the board, he bumps into a trio of Oriental tourists just arriving to his left. There are apologies all round. Lawrence envies them the simplicity and superficiality of their search.

~

"Tilt. Is it?"

There is something a little more insistent in the tone now, as if this second version of me - who, by the way, is rapidly climbing the pain-in-the-arse scale - will seemingly not shut-up until I have answered his damned question. And how should I do that? Go back into the BL and see if Duncan is still there - after all he will be alone now. Or perhaps make my way to the Adelphi and try and talk some sense into the management there?

The notion of going to Foyles comes at me from left-field. Perhaps that talk of books - first with Justin and then, internally, about my relationship with fiction - has resurrected the ghosts of other conversations, their residue imprinted on my synapses. Weighing up the notion, I wonder if such a visit might help take the question away. I could go to the plays section and see where my book will reside once Justin eventually gets off his backside and tells Kelsey to make it happen. Or even - and here's an idea which is so remote and unexpected that it's in another parish! - I could go and see where my fiction would sit were I ever to master it. Between Thackeray and Tolkien, perhaps? Strange bedfellows indeed! Persuading myself it might be fun, I check my coffee and my watch one more time, then stand. "I think taxi, don't you, Tilt, Old Man?"

After a short but thoroughly dissatisfying stop-start journey, the taxi drops me across the road from Foyles. Assuming my next cabbie will choose to venture up Tottenham Court Road when returning to King's Cross does nothing to soothe me as I know that journey is likely to be a far more hideous experience. I despise Tottenham Court Road with a passion even if it is a little irrational to do so. It has always struck me as one of those semi-shabby streets which perpetually fails to make up its mind as to what it is supposed to be. From my perspective it's a grubby, noisy, over-populated thoroughfare whose purpose has crystallised solely to facilitate journeys from one end of it to the other, from Oxford Street to Euston Road. Standing facing Foyles and waiting for a gap in the traffic, I know for many people Charing Cross Road is little better, some might even say worse; but at least it has the Garrick and the Phoenix, and I was once propositioned by a prostitute on Charing Cross Road. So it also has that - a vestige of memory and anecdote - in its favour.

Standing immediately inside the entrance to the bookshop, I pause and take a breath, almost as if it were possible to inhale something - greatness, wisdom - from the shelves, contributions to top-up those same qualities already in my possession. Glancing to my right, I see a woman in her mid-forties do exactly the same thing. From the look on her face you could be forgiven for thinking she had entered a temple and was about to pay homage to her god. Which she may well be, of course. And me? I walk down the treads of the curved staircase and recall how the place used to be. Not that I'm one of those who still hankers after the traditional old Foyles with its cramped darkness, the tellers in their little wood-and-glass booths, the bizarre rituals involved when buying a book. I welcomed the news when I found out they'd gutted the place, opened it up, made it light and airy and welcoming. It had been transformed into a place where you could suddenly find what you were looking for - and discover what you didn't know you needed. There is modernity in its reimagining, and as I walk further into the shop and toward the lifts I wonder if Foyles hasn't already experienced a journey parallel to that upon which I am about to embark. If *Rust* is the future, a radical departure from the past, then might Foyles stand as a metaphor for what I am about to do with my work, to open it out and let in the light?

"Is it?"

As I look at the store guide on the wall, the nagging voice prompts the cloud settle again, almost as if the old bookshop was still there haunting the present.

'Drama, Plays, Theatre': floor two. And then I notice 'Fiction/ Literature': floor one. I wonder how such a pecking order is arrived at, novels located within easiest reach for the punters. Presumably the geography is commercially-driven. Although far from ideal, I recognise it could be worse for my own milieu than to reside on the second floor. It might well have been banished to the fourth along with Biology, Computing, Engineering, Law; a location where - inexplicably mixed in with the sciences - Drama might sit cheek-by-jowl with the

Dictionaries already there. Surely the fabric upon which this entire edifice is built - words and their definitions - should be front and centre, not relegated to a cobwebbed corner somewhere behind Maths and Physics? As I examine the floor guide, I sense multiple pairs of eyes flitting about the place, mainly examining not just the contents of the shelves but also fellow book-worshippers. It's almost as if, in a place such as this, it is not merely the books that are on display. Browsing par excellence. Confident I look the part, as if I belong here, I am suitably comforted not to need to reevaluate my appearance in the light of this general scrutiny, and eschew the lift in favour of the stairs. It is only one floor after all.

It takes no time at all for me to recognise that the majority of the bustle is confined to the ground floor. 'Footfall' is the term, I believe. I daresay the differential between where I now stand and the arena where people never make it beyond 'Best Sellers', Fiction in general, and the detritus of spin-offs and 'literary' materials such as notebooks and pens, is considerable. I am reminded of the shop at the British Library. Although it is difficult to draw an exact parallel between the two and thus to quantify their respective degrees of 'dumbing down', I know which I prefer. Away from the ground level and first floor busyness there is something strangely comforting and peaceful about the second floor. Reflective even. From where I pause near the stairs I can see perhaps six or seven others nearby, each adopting various poses, though almost all bent to a degree, head down, hands cradling a volume of one sort or another. Settled by this, I follow the signs to the drama section and soon find myself standing in front of a bank of shelves, the vast majority of which are dominated by Shakespeare. The Ts begin soon after and I quickly locate where my own volume will reside: apparently between Peter Terson and Ben Travers. I have heard of Travers, and of Terson's 'Zigger, Zagger', but that is as far as it goes. Under such circumstances - and given I have the advantage of having my 'finger on the pulse' as it were - then surely when the name 'Tilt' appears between those two, and in the bold font I have suggested Justin uses, well... A standout edition. Even if my newly arrived second voice might disagree, there will be something comforting in that. Mission accomplished.

Before retreating downstairs to undertake a similar study in the more crowded field of fiction, I find an empty seat near the lifts and decide to sit for a few minutes just to observe. Observation: one of the essential tools of my trade. I watch people in order to steal them, to whisk them away and locate them in a new environment, to gift them a new life - which may be a better or worse one than that they currently inhabit. If only they knew! And if they did, and if it were in my power to allow them to choose between the two, presumably they would universally seek the better, always wanting to be rewarded with more or less of something? I watch a young man as he strides down the stairs. Engineering type. A candidate from the fourth floor if ever I saw one. I wonder what I could do with his life, how I might reconcile his past and present, define his future. There is something in the way he walks which reminds me of Morgan Stubbs; an unwelcome intrusion given I am trying to reestablish my normally perfect equilibrium. Trying to lighten the mood by playfully regarding that missing sense of balance as if it were a child's lost toy, I try and recall when I last saw it. Arriving at Kings's Cross, perhaps? Or just before I entered the British Library? I recall the walk, the Shaw theatre - and there is Morgan Stubbs once again. Given what happened over coffee, the last thing I need is to think about Stubbs. Magda lost her equilibrium in *The Discomforted* and look what happened to her! It is a fate I have no wish to share.

I look back to the stairs and find the young man has disappeared. If only Stubbs had been expunged from my life as easily and painlessly. But he had been difficult to deal with. My relative youth didn't help - especially as that's what he had been counting on to engineer what appeared to be a good deal for me. Smoke and mirrors. That his post-*Discomforted* proposal was an especially brilliant deal for him came out soon enough. He hadn't counted on my already razor-sharp insight to ferret that out in double-quick time. Perhaps he had assumed it would be easy for him to milk me for as long as possible before I was inevitably picked up by a competent agent. Which I assumed was Duncan.

"Is it?"

The same question assails me from an undefinable elsewhere, though as it seems to be layered with a different context this time I can only regard it as less threatening - especially as I realise my subconscious mind formed my previous thought in the past tense: 'which I assumed *was* Duncan'. *Is* Duncan the man? No doubt he has questions to answer. After all, he was responsible for introducing me to Justin; and although that seemed fortuitous at the time, there are evidently problems in that department. Why, for example, did Duncan not leap to my defence over coffee? On reflection, he was unhelpfully silent. This is not an issue I would have expected to be entertaining when I disembarked from the train just over two hours ago.

Seeking diversion, I glance around and settle on the stairs once more. An intermittent stream of people heading in both directions parade before me, as if they are auditioning to make a contribution of some kind to my next play, that which will follow *Rust*. Not that I have any concrete ideas as to how I'm going to improve on that little masterpiece. Not yet, anyway. However, my meeting with Duncan and Justin - plus the off-stage interference from the masters of the Adelphi - have only served to further convince me that I shouldn't go back to a simple rehash of my old stuff, and that I must push on, go further. Even as I was writing it, I knew *Rust* was merely scratching the surface, an Expeditionary Force into new territory.

"Is it?"

"Yes, it is" I would like to tell this annoying, nagging, second-me voice. I'd love to enter into a dialogue with it - no an argument! - to make my case. But all I can do is distract it.

The head of a man appears as he ascends the stairs, closely followed by that of a woman. Soon it is clear they are hand-in-hand, absorbed in mutual proximity, by the bubble in which they seem to be existing. I could lift them and place them on any staircase in the world and it would make no difference to how they are at this precise moment. Love, of course. I have considered a foray back into a romantic theme - though one with an element of *Rust* about it. In all senses of the word. An honest portrait of the emotion, if you will. Something sharp and new and inventive; a play that asks the questions everyone wants to ask but are seldom prepared to articulate; or a piece populated by 'in love' characters who say exactly what they want to say exactly when they want to say it, unfettered by convention and social mores. And if I did, would a couple such as these two love-birds now climbing out of my sight be in the starring roles? Hardly. When love is as fresh and new as it obviously is in their case - irrespective of their ages and whether or not they should know better - it would be churlish to destroy it too soon. Perhaps impossible. No, I would need other characters, cut from an entirely different cloth. Like Mimi. And me.

Although I have no desire to recall her nor resuscitate memories of our eventually toxic relationship, I cannot help but wonder where she is now and whether, were she to walk past me right at this minute, I would still recognise her. There were rumours of facelifts and botox after I left her. Presumably trying to make herself more appealing to a younger model. God knows she'd been trying that for long enough - in fact as soon as the gloss had begun to wear off our sordid little entanglement. Not that was how it started of course. "Tilt, don't get maudlin…" What does that mean, exactly? Maudlin? Not really my bag. But I remember those early days and walks along the Thames, across the railway bridge at Charing Cross and then to the South Bank; the dreadful *Richard II* we saw, or that bizarre Spanish offering at the NFT. It was blissful in the way it was supposed to be - and the kind of thing my new play (were I to write about love) would ruthlessly expose. But how to do so? Well, not to pull any punches on sex for a start! To unravel that little web of lies we weave for ourselves when we mistake a good shag for something more ethereal, something worthy of a different and more refined name. I confess Mimi was rather splendid in that department. You'd imagine so from her name, wouldn't you? Easy to see her as a courtesan-type, short skirts and high heels, loitering in the doorways of the Rue St. Denis. Allegedly.

Not that I was a slouch between the sheets either. "Tilt, you old rogue!" At least that's what Amanda used to say. I know it's the kind of thing a woman says early doors in order to stroke a man's ego, but to give Amanda her due she kept the flattery up for quite a while. If you were to press me, I'd say a few years actually. Was it fortunate or unfortunate that she overlapped with Mimi for a little while? Some people made too much of that - especially Mimi. She had her reasons I suppose. But from my perspective Amanda freed me from the prison Mimi seemed intent on building. I think Mimi had created this image of herself: the famous playwright's wife, the power behind the throne. She saw nothing but a life of premieres and champagne - a life I was supposed to deliver on a plate. Amanda had no such ambitions, happy to leave all that spotlight malarkey to me; which was one of the other things I liked about her. Well, more than liked, obviously. However, the present question under the microscope is whether or not I could find a place for a Mimi- or Amanda-like character in my new play. If I did, I'd have to find an angle; in Amanda's case, compromise her true character in order to avoid the saccharine and sentimental. Strange how I still manage to regard her with as much fondness as I do, especially given how she left me.

"Is it?"

Is it what, I wonder. Is there strangeness in my residual fondness for her in spite of the fact that she left me - and her reasons for doing so? She knew what she was buying into, that's all I'll say. I was already an established entity when she met me; more so when she walked out five years later, blaming me for becoming intolerable. Something I never accepted, of course. Wasn't I simply an innocent victim of Covid? Theatres being closed, I was theoretically forced to remain holed-up in one location for weeks at a time. I'll admit Amanda adapted better than I did, but then there was always something of the pragmatic about her, in spite of those heady romantic overtones. I may have been something of a 'refusenik', but there were principles involved - and I simply couldn't rattle around doing nothing. I needed to be me, the man I'd become. All of that upset her, undermined her; she thought I was either going too far or not going far enough. Yes, I flouted the rules from time to time, who didn't? And yes, I had the fines to prove it. But at least she hadn't been aware of the Soho assignations which had accompanied to them… They were escapades I still like to think of as research. It was as if, even then, I knew that there would be *Rust* - and then potentially something following it, something related to that rag-bag of emotion we call 'love'. Which all fits rather nicely, doesn't it? Even down to that age-old cliché about a man suffering for his art.

From my perch I see the stairs are quiet, and behind me there are just three people milling about. One of them is hovering near the Shakespeare and I can't help but wonder whether there is *always* someone there, and whether the carpet isn't worn just a little thinner at that point. 'The Shakespeare'. How much did he become the image of himself, I wonder; playwright above all else. That famous signature, like a brand. A single word that in and of itself has come to mean so much, has told a story as well as any of his plays. And I can't help but think of 'TILT' drafted in a bold and remarkable font, perhaps slightly embossed on the cover of my book; writ large on post-*Rust* theatre posters. Perhaps I could help design a new font, just for the purpose. Will that word become a similar conveyance of meaning? It does, after all, say so much about me already. In spite of what Duncan said - and what that weasel Justin implied - I like to think it has a certain weight; a cachet, if you will. The little adventure we went on after *The Discomforted* built up the momentum, and with momentum came more bums on seats, longer runs, more money. There was - and here I can't help but smile to myself, shooting benevolence into the air of Foyles - even public anticipation. "What next? What next?" Eventually *Rust* was next - though it too proved another victim of Covid with the theatres just back, fewer people, and most wanting easy-going happiness. Perhaps they saw 'TILT' on the posters and made assumptions based on past experience: they were going into a safe environment, knew what to expect. And *Rust* was anything but. It was never meant to be. More bad timing than a balloon bursting, that's what I should have said to Duncan. Isn't it all about timing? If the Adelphi wanted happy punters who didn't have to engage their brains then they should have put on *The Sound of Music* or Agatha Christie. Bad timing, that's all. The simple equation where Tilt equalled money in the bank became unresolvable because someone - some *thing* - had changed the rules of engagement. But they'll see. Let them take it off if they want to. Give me six to twelve months, a new theatre, perhaps a new Duncan - who knows? - and *Rust* will be back. And in my pocket I'll have the next masterpiece almost ready to go. They'll need a bigger font on their posters for that one!

A sudden increase in noise forces me to rise, go to the walkway railing, and look down into the atrium. A small party of mid-teens has arrived trailing disconsolately behind a rattled teacher. What if they were to look up, see me here, and someone said "Isn't that that guy? You know, the one wot wrote thingy..." And the teacher might say, "Why yes, that's Tilt..." and they'd gallop up the stairs seeking autographs, the teacher apologising for the intrusion, fulsome in her praise for my work, grateful that I'd saved her little bookstore field-trip. But no-one looks up - or if they do, there is no recognition. And when I lose sight of them as they head noisily for the lifts - perhaps destined for the fourth floor - the notion of waiting six to twelve months to see *Rust* resurrected comes back to me, time stretching into the future like a chasm. That long? Really? Surely too long to wait, too long out of the limelight?

"Is it?"

Making my way to the stairs I wonder whether plays and playwrights are artistically radioactive and have a half-life of some kind - especially playwrights! - and if so, whether my clock has started ticking, wound-up by Duncan, Justin and the bloody Adelphi. There's no knowing how long it might keep going: ten years, five years? I need to get *Rust* back on stage somewhere in six months, max. And I need to get down to business with the love idea. Perhaps I have to be more Tilt during the next few months than I've ever been; be seen, do interviews. Maybe the BBC would be interested in me doing 'Dessert Island Discs'. Or an 'Arena' special with Alan Yentob. That would work. Has Duncan got the wherewithal to fix either of those? Heading down to the ground floor I feel a brief wave of excitement, elation even; but then turning to face into the yards and yards of fiction I find myself daunted by a prospect I struggle to name. There suddenly seems little point in trying to work out exactly where a novel by Tilt would sit; somewhere between Thackeray and Tolstoy of course, but where precisely? And does it matter? The realisation that I will never successfully put pen to paper in that way hits me like a slap round the face. Yes, the competition is ridiculously severe, but I've always assumed - until this moment - that my theatrical track record would give me a head start, a foot in the door. A door my name had opened. Then I think again of Justin, unable to erase him from my short-term memory. What was it I just thought? "I'll never put pen to paper in that way"? 'Tilt' and 'never' are two variables which fail to compute, which shouldn't appear together in the same construct. And yet there they are, drafted into consciousness by the lead player himself, the star of the show, almost as if he had forgotten his lines and had chosen to make something up - anything - in order to keep the momentum of thinking going. Distracted, I turn on my well-heeled heels to face away from the many thousands of made-up stories and accidentally bump into an elderly woman who's just heading towards them. I smile, flash the opportunity of recognition at her, but she mumbles gruffly and heads into make-believe. Moments later I am back on Charing Cross Road, checking my watch. Not even one o'clock yet.

Glancing up the road to where Tottenham Court Road threatens, a wave of disappointment assails me; not simply due the prospect of TCR (a prospect which instinctively makes me turn and walk away from it), but also with time and how it has passed today. And then, scrambling to be piled on top of that discomfort, further layers of disappointment comprising of Duncan, Justin, our meeting, the book, the Adelphi. Even Mimi and Amanda manage to edge their way in. Mimi was always one for taking advantage of a situation, especially any opportunity for kicking a man when he's down. I've seen her in action. Felt her in action more than once. All unwelcome, they have suddenly ganged up on me, these faces, time; bullies of the first order. Having the urge to fight back, as I walk on I try to concentrate on the next six months and what I need to be doing - but even then my mind wanders. As if by some preordained coincidence, at this precise moment I happen to glance to my right and into the doorway of what used to be a run-down X-rated cinema, the doorway from which that diminutive prostitute emerged all those years ago, sidling up to me, walking close but not touching, staring up into my face before she began to zig-zag wildly across the pavement, trying to make me stop, to say something, because then she knew she'd have at least a part of me in her grasp. I try to smile. She would be good in a play, a character like that; provide another slant on 'love' and what it meant. Or didn't mean. Even now I wonder whether or not I should have stopped, confronted her, seen what happened. But I had been younger then, not the Tilt I am today. And if it happened again, right here, right now? I check the doorway once more but carry on walking, trying to distract myself by watching the crowd, listening to the backing track of London traffic, the punctuation of shouts, voices of people who pass by allowing me to catch fragments of their conversations. Perhaps there is something there, in that fragmentary interception, I could use; it would, after all, offer so much scope for understanding and misunderstanding.

13:00

Toby resumes his walk and heads back to where the rounders game had been in progress. He finds himself needing to close out the Bolsover memory, to wrap it up and hide it away. As he passes a waste bin he wishes he could dispose of it forever.

It was unusual for wives to accompany the team on their 'tours'. Unusual, but not unknown. Exceptions were made based on the potential gatecrasher's knowledge of the local area, what might be loosely termed their 'connections', and whether they were prepared to act as scorer in at least one of the games. The latter was the usual 'fee'. Huw's long-suffering wife Sandi had been the most frequent non-playing attendee. Not only had she proven herself an exemplary recorder (the neatness of her scorebook pages stood out from all the others), it could be fun having her around in the evenings, her slightly 'Home Counties' glamour and outgoing personality adding a little variety to what might otherwise descend into puerile drinking bouts. From what Toby had previously seen, she had earned 'a reputation' based on little more than circumstantial evidence. It was a potential blemish Huw brushed off with a resigned shrug of the shoulders - and which Sandi occasionally chose to play up to, in spite of him. Toby had assumed it was show, bravado, ego; her simply longing to be the centre of attention. Until Bolsover.

Reaching the junction between the Inner Circle and York Bridge, Toby pauses, ostensibly to decide on which way to go back to Euston Road. However as he does so he finds himself simultaneously juggling with the notion that he was almost certainly not Sandi's only conquest. This not being his first confrontation with that conclusion - how could it have been?! - it hits him hard every time, and once again he mentally scans the dressing room to see if he can identify other potential partners, willing or otherwise. Matthew? Probably. Dan? Perhaps not. Does it bother him not being the first? Or not being the only? Or not the last? Or is most significance garnered from the fact that the encounter happened at all? Toby knows he has never been very good at working through the obscure, always preferring the concrete (like the feel of a Dukes ball in his hand!) and failing that, the certainty and loyalty of numbers. But as far as the subtleties and ambiguities of relationships are concerned? He believes he has known Marita for long enough to shift her into the 'concrete' category. The excitement of their emotional adventure is now long in the past, and - from his perspective at least - something he has grown out of. Is that how she feels too? Yet now, persistently lurking in the background, is the episode with Sandi and about which surely Marita knows nothing. If she were faced with the truth of it, how might she react? Does his concrete knowledge of her extend that far?

Until this moment Toby believes he has never considered he might lose her too. Cricket, his job, Marita. A holy trinity. Rather than being a man standing at the edge of Euston Road, he suddenly feels as if he is on the edge of a precipice, one step from oblivion.

He checks his watch. Not yet one-fifteen. His train is at three. Toby tries to focus on the potential of the next hour and forty-five minutes: sufficient time to do something tangible, yet too little to do anything meaningful. Looking to his right he gauges the distance to Baker Street station, calculates how long it will take him to get there, and then the duration of the tube ride to King's Cross. Without doubt commencing such a journey now would leave him with the best part of an hour to kill at the station, an unappealing prospect. He looks down at his crutch, measuring the pressure his hand is applying to it as if that might be a sign of something. His heel aches a little, but not debilitatingly so. Given he has managed to walk further than he had anticipated, perhaps he will walk east a little while longer; perhaps to Goodge Street, just to see how he gets on.

~

Imogen's exit from the building is considerably less time-consuming than her entrance. Bypassing the convoluted mechanisms of entry security, her final encounter is with a lone Shard employee standing at an isolated desk where they collect visitors' passes and indicate the exit doors. Once outside, Imogen checks her watch: it is a little before one o'cock. She has allowed herself plenty of time to have lunch before she needs to think about getting back to King's Cross. Finding St. Thomas' Street looks exactly as it had two hours earlier, she knows nothing will have changed in Borough Market either. Working through her options, Imogen rules out getting something to eat at London Bridge station as quickly as she does giving the market a second chance. These disqualifications seem to leave her no choice other than to go hunting somewhere else, almost as unattractive an option as those she has already ruled out. Then she remembers the coffee shop she has already patronised offered a menu of sorts. The lesser of all the evils on offer.

When her panini arrives less than twenty minutes later - placed in front of her on the same table at which she had previously sat - she is surprised to find it garnished with a little fresh salad and a few crinkle-cut crisps. Even before she has tried it, the presentation alone seems sufficient to justify her decision. She smiles at the barista who delivered it.

"Thank you. It looks great."

Cutting her sandwich into six more manageable chunks, Imogen inevitably replays her hour-long experience in The Shard. From where she sits she can only make out a small number of the upper floors, the buildings in-between shielding its lower portion. Taking a bite of her beef and horseradish panini, she is instantly grateful she chose that over ham and cheese.

On balance she thought the interview had gone pretty well, and she is confident there had been a connection with Anthony. Of Alistair she is less sure, and his question about 'deliverables' comes back to her. Had she been right to take the tack she had and place herself more in Sonia's shoes than her own? It had allowed her maintain momentum for sure, and demonstrated - to herself, if not her interlocutors - her potential, what she was capable of. Should it have been a surprise that, once in the groove, she had found the impersonation easy? There had been times during the annual appraisal process when Sonia had suggested Imogen possessed a certain 'bossiness'. Imogen smiles and takes another bite. She's not sure that is the exact word Sonia had used, but the message seemed to be that - very occasionally - she could be a little intolerant of others and far too keen to demonstrate her superiority. All complete rubbish, of course; she was simply doing her job. Imogen knew she did not suffer fools gladly, but what was she supposed to do when they got in her way or hindered her getting on? "Things can be misinterpreted", Sonia had once said, somewhat cryptically; Imogen had wondered who was doing the misinterpreting. As far as she was concerned she got on well with the other members of Sonia's team. Although working in diverse parts of the business they were in the same boat, trying to do pretty much the same job, achieve the same things. Why shouldn't she share the benefit of her experience with her colleagues to help them along, even if it meant appearing to disagree with Sonia herself on occasion? They were a good team and if Sonia couldn't see that, well, such shortsightedness represented more of a failure on her part than anyone else's.

She is just about to pick up the penultimate slice of her panini when she hears her phone ringing in her bag. Lifting it out, she unlocks it and checks the number. London.

"This is Imogen," she says, slipping into her best EA-voice.

"Imogen, hi. Arabella Hardy."

The other voice is crisp but friendly, and striving to sound older than the person who owns it. Imogen processes it for a fraction of a second before assigning it to the recruitment agent.

"Arabella."

"They've come back to me," Arabella says, almost in code.

"Already? That was quick. Anthony said they didn't mess about - which is good, isn't it? Must have been an easy decision for them."

There is a moment as Imogen looks down to her plate, her half-eaten sandwich, then outside to the bustle of Borough High Street; a moment when she begins to propel herself forward into a life where this café is a regular haunt, this table, this view.

"I'm afraid it's a 'no'."

Arabella's words slap her around the face.

"'No'?" Imogen wonders if someone has been changing lexical definitions while she hasn't been looking.

"They said it was good to meet you and they enjoyed the interview etcetera, but you didn't quite have what they were looking for. One of the other candidates was a far closer match."

"In what way wasn't I what they wanted?"

"From what I can gather, Anthony didn't think you quite had enough of the EA-experience he was looking for; that you needed a few more years." When Imogen says nothing, Arabella carries on. "You *did* know the job was to be his own EA? They told you that, right?"

Imogen, in a tailspin, tries to remember whether they had said any such thing.

"I mean, I didn't know myself until just now," Arabella says, trying to excuse any personal culpability, "so it wasn't like I didn't tell you or anything. Maybe they thought they'd get more genuine responses from candidates if they didn't know." Her voice trails away for a moment.

"They didn't say," Imogen says. "Not even a hint." She thinks of the 'deliverables' question, then rules it out.

"Well, plenty more fish in the sea…" Arabella tries to sound upbeat. "We've got your details of course, and now that we have a better idea of what you're after I'm sure we'll be able to help you out soon."

And then Arabella is gone.

Absent-mindedly placing her phone on the table, Imogen looks again at the view outside. London suddenly seems grubbier, over-crowded, more run-down. The door to the street opens as someone enters allowing sound to flood in, an unorchestrated cacophony. Hard on its heels, she is assaulted by echoes of the brief conversation with Arabella: "not enough EA-experience", "needed a few more years", "genuine responses". And "no". What is she supposed to do with any of that, words from a script she has not expected to be played out before her? Alastair's question nags at her too, and she recalls how she'd handled it. Pretending to be Sonia; didn't that automatically endow her with more experience, a greater number of years? Hadn't she demonstrated how much she had understood of what needed to be done - of what she was capable of doing?

Almost instantly her failure becomes Sonia's fault. If Sonia had been a better manager and role-model then surely that would have rubbed off on her? Imogen computes that she had failed the interview not because of any flaws on her part, but because the profile she had tried to duplicate was an inadequate one; it was as if the mirror she had looked into had been cracked or bloomed. If she is angry it is not with herself for choosing such a template but more with Sonia for letting her down. How can she respect her manager after this? When she returns to work tomorrow and Sonia calls her into her office, how will she feel when she looks across the desk at her? Will she regard her current boss through a lens of insufficient experience and "needing more years"? If so, she imagines any doubts she may have previously held about Sonia will solidify before her eyes - and that will tell her something.

"How is everything?"

The barista's voice shakes her from her reverie; the young woman glances down with concern at Imogen's unfinished panini.

"Yes, fine." The barista doesn't move. "I mean, the panini's great. I was just on the phone."

"Ah, okay. If you need anything else, just give me a shout." Evidently relieved, the woman smiles and moves to the next table where she starts clearing the detritus left by its previous occupants.

Imogen wonders about the barista's own experience and age, and tries to imagine what it's like being her and working here, whether she enjoys her job, what there is outside of Borough High Street that keeps her going. These are questions which immediately bounce back to her from the same imperfect mirror that, just a moment ago, held Sonia's image. Half-heartedly, Imogen picks up the penultimate slice of her sandwich and bites into it; expecting more flavour, it now seems unaccountably bland. Even her lunch is betraying her. Because that's how it feels, betrayal: by Sonia for being an inadequate model; by Arabella for her incomplete portrayal of the job; by a combination of Alastair and Anthony in terms of their manipulation of her. If that was how Alistair worked - asking difficult questions on the back of not being honest about the role - then perhaps she'd had a lucky escape after all. Even if she had liked Anthony.

She wonders why she should stop there. Why not go back nearly twenty years to when Louise and Emma went off to university leaving her at home with their parents? Or three years later when the two of them briefly returned from college only to then disappear permanently? Or the year after that - as if given permission to finally admit to some dark secret -

the divorce of her parents and her father's departure, that somehow inevitable climax which consigned her and her mother to their lonely lives together? Surely those were the betrayals which made up the foundations of her present life, cementing in place the disappointment from which she has been struggling to free herself ever since. Even Lee - who just six years ago teased her with the hope that he might just be the one to release her - name and all - found the task too daunting. Perhaps she had been cursed and Lee, at the eleventh hour, recognised how he too would be tainted if he took her on. They all had a part to play.

Biting hard into the last of her beef and horseradish, teeth tearing into the bread as if she was on a revenge mission, Imogen knows the scale of today's treachery is insignificant compared to Lee's. She tries to tell herself than in a week she will be over Alistair and Anthony, and that Arabella may well have lined up another interview for her. But Lee? Even if she continues to tell herself she is over him, part of her knows the contrary is true. Which is something else the unrelenting attachment of her name represents: the ongoing proof of his abandonment of her.

At first she had tried to persuade him that all he was feeling was a case of 'cold feet'. She believed it was typical for a man to go through such a phase a few months in advance of 'tying the knot' - even if he hadn't yet explicitly made it to the threshold of proposal. There was a window for him doing so, and Imogen knew it was open. Having known Lee for five years already, she was well aware how his mind worked, how he processed things. She had mapped out their future thoroughly, leaving a trail of clues for him to follow. Some of these had been explicit, such as the relevance of her gifts or the enhanced sophistication in celebratory events such as birthdays and Christmas. She had ensured their holidays began to test out various components she might want to include on a honeymoon; and unbeknownst to him, they explored places which were candidates for that ultimate destination - only for her to rule them out one by one. And he had gone along with all of her explicit and implicit planning, increasingly submissive to her suggestions; all of which could only mean that he was edging closer to posing the ultimate question.

Yet he had been doing no such thing. Rather, he had been buying time as he planned his escape, digging a metaphorical tunnel in plain sight. And she had failed to see it. That last day when he said he wanted to talk to her about something important and suggested they go for a walk, Imogen assumed her moment had arrived. Given it was a regular haunt of theirs - indeed the place where he had first kissed her all those years before - his choice of the local country park seemed perfect, even romantic. They had walked by the lake and he had steered her to a bench near where swans and their cygnets swam harmoniously. With a sudden rush of satisfaction and anticipation, she felt he *had* been paying attention after all; as if he had finally understood how *she* worked, what made her tick, what she wanted. She had waited, heart beating, for the moment when he slipped from the bench to one knee and pulled the ring box from his fleece pocket...

But he had simply looked out onto the lake - into the distance, not even at the swans - and began with "I'm sorry...". Moments later her script had been in tatters. He had chosen a public place not in homage to prior associations, but to minimise the chance of a scene; there was no kneeling, no ring box. Just an apology and a half-hearted confession she still struggles to recall word-for-word, her focus having been shattered as soon as he had uttered the words "break up". What else had he said? That there was no-one else; that she was a wonderful person; that she was too good for him. Well-rehearsed lines. Instead of reading a book about wedding speeches, Lee had found an alternative volume to consult.

She hadn't been as angry then as she was now. It was an anger which had grown slowly and cancerously across the intervening years. Seeing a couple walking hand-in-hand across the road from her, Imogen wants to rush out into the High Street, dodge the streams of traffic, and shake the woman free, begging she run before it is too late. She would be telling a complete stranger to do what she herself had been powerless to do years before - because why would you run from your dreams?

After a few moments he had left her there, sitting alone, abandoned - just as Arabella had done via the phone, or Anthony at the lifts with that half-seen gesture. Or Louise and Emma - and by them more than once. Her eyes had remained fixed on the swans as they continued to float in front of her, serene, oblivious, unaffected. She hadn't even watched him walk away. From somewhere there had come a shout, the bark of a dog. To the rest of the world it was an unremarkable day. As was today.

But it hadn't been, of course; then or now. Not for her. She had returned home only after wandering the park for far too long, an activity undertaken ostensibly to give her the chance to process what Lee had said - and unconsciously to give him the opportunity to make good on his escape. Getting back to the house and finding him in mid-flight would hardly have been good for either of them. As she walked up to the front door (his car nowhere to be seen) she hoped she was already beginning to edit him out of her life, yet she discovered the house almost unchanged. Wandering through the downstairs rooms in something of a trance, she was unable not to imagine she had dreamed the whole thing: they hadn't gone to the park; he hadn't said what he'd said; she'd not been left there alone with just the swans for company. It was only when she got upstairs and discovered his clothes were gone that she began to notice other absences: shoes, coats, his laptop, a few books. Then a little while later, his favourite two mugs from the kitchen. As a collection, it didn't seem much to represent the last few years they had lived together. All that remained had always felt more hers than his anyway, things she had chosen or insisted they buy, the residue from their shopping expeditions manifested in items which had her fingerprints indelibly etched on them. Would he be back to collect more? She had looked at the sofa and for a brief second tried to see him walk through the door with a chainsaw determined to rescue his half, the half nearest the television, presumably along with the side table on which he had liked to keep the remote control, his beer. But that was ridiculous.

After a surprisingly good sleep, when she had come downstairs the following morning she looked round to find not only that she was alone, but that Lee's departure had been no more significant than had a lodger moved out. She searched for evidence of a misplaced future, as if she would find new voids where that future had once been embodied in now removed physical objects; she searched, but found none. Did that mean they had never been there in the first place? Or that her future with Lee had been no more than an illusion?

So she went to work the next day pretending nothing had changed; going through the motions just as Lee had been for those last few days, or weeks, or months. How was she to measure how long he had been deceiving her?

Finishing the last of her coffee and registering that the woman on Borough High Street she had wanted to save was now out of sight - and therefore lost - Imogen can only remember the rest of that first non-Lee week in vague emotional terms. She had been out-of-kilter, she knew that; slightly grumpy, slightly officious. By the Thursday morning she had felt the coming weekend looming large like an monolith over which she had no influence or control - and which she would need to tackle on her own. By the end of the afternoon she had rationalised those fears away and turned it into a challenge, something she could plan for, plough through. Then, when she got home from work, she found letters on the doormat addressed to 'Miss I. Mansfield'. Seeing her name spelled out in that way made everything unravel once again.

Looking down and finding both plate and cup empty, Imogen checks the time. Just before two o'clock. She had given herself the option of fitting in a little shopping before heading back to King's Cross; but she has taken longer than expected over lunch, derailed by Arabella's call and the subsequent need to process its fall-out. She had not planned for that, nor the unwanted intrusion of the spectre of Lee. Of course, Arabella's responsibility didn't stretch that far. In a way Lee had been with her when she had entered The Shard, as had Louise and Emma. Standing up, she wonders whether she will ever be able to shake them off.

At the counter she gives the barista a generous smile in an attempt to back-up what she had said earlier about her lunch, then flicks her credit card at the scanner. Another 'beep', just like The Shard security machine, the ping of the lifts. More echoes. Out on the pavement she looks at her watch again then up at the building not so far away now as it towers over the city. She tries to recall the view from the seventeenth floor, the expanse of the station, the sprawl extending to the horizon. Was that London then: all of that plus a compendium made up of streets like this or St. Thomas's, taxis and buses, people walking arm-in-arm, joggers dressed in unnatural colours, the grime in the gutters and doorways, the pigeons everywhere, and the essence of something else upon which she is unable to put her finger? And if so, is it a compilation to which she could attach herself, invest in its promises and dreams? Did it really reflect her in any way - either the Imogen she was now or the one she wanted to be? Three hours earlier she had known the answer, but now, as she heads towards London Bridge station, she is not so sure.

~

Lawrence, momentarily thrown, checks his watch. One o'clock. Still two hours before his train is due to leave. Having become unsettled, he continues to head east attempting to succumb to the distraction of his surroundings: the path, the river, the joggers in their brightly-coloured sportswear. Without further incident, a few minutes later he has passed under both Southwark Bridge and the railway crossing leading to Canon Street Station on the northern side of the river. Here the sounds of trains passing overhead are more muffled than they had been at Charing Cross. For a short period Lawrence loses sight of the river as the path leads him between buildings, the ground floor of many having been converted into restaurants or cafés or bijou shopping experiences. He is tempted by coffee once again but finds the residue of two lattes still sufficiently strong to dissuade him. As the buildings either side of him give way, he encounters a crowd of sightseers gathered around the perimeter of a replica of the 'Golden Hind'; many are taking selfies. They seem unconcerned that the ship is a modern reconstruction of Drake's vessel, and even those bothering to read the information boards to make that discovery remain enthusiastic. Camera phones click near-silently but incessantly, and Lawrence finds himself captivated not by the ship but by those around it. He finds a suitable location a little way removed to stand and observe. To anyone coming across him at that moment he would appear as no more than a face in the crowd.

Yet it is not anonymity he seeks but identity. He longs to be recognised again. The meeting with Dylan and Tessa had been a start, but their acknowledgement of him was always likely to be conditional, lack meaningful scale. As far as his mother had been concerned his importance to her was without question. Had he not been her staff for so many years, and she his? After Dylan and then Tessa left home - not to mention his father - who else did she have to lean on? But when he abandoned her, what did that do for her feelings towards him? He looks at this pristine new ship yet can only think of the original, presumably now a wreck elsewhere. Was that what he had become to her during those painful last months? Did he place her in a situation where all she could do was to reconstruct a mental imagine of him knowing the real Lawrence was elsewhere? He wonders about this fake 'Golden Hind' and whether it would be capable of undertaking the same journey as the original. He doubts it. And if that's what he too had become - a cheap replicant of the person he had once been - how could that bode well?

Dylan clearly judged the post-mother Lawrence as inadequate, yet perhaps Tessa still hoped that enough of her original brother might yet remain. And he himself? What did he see when he looked in the mirror, the original or the fake? Finding he cannot possibly know, he wants to be told, to be guided, to be steered. Having had that luxury for a short while, he wants it back.

Trapped between the river and the milling crowd, Lawrence finds he needs more space. Setting off with the air of a man who has suddenly realised he is late for an appointment, he marches through the crowd as if he knows where he is going. At the head of the dry dock and turning slightly to his left, he comes across a sign indicating that Borough Market is away to his right. However its message fails to register given that immediately in front of him - almost as if it is located there for his benefit alone - the edifice of Southwark Cathedral rises against the sky. Had he known it was here? He is unsure. Yet if he had - subconsciously at least - is it not possible this is where he has been heading all along, ever since that day those few weeks ago when Dylan suggested the South Bank for their meeting, after which he had subsequently traced out what he might do subsequently? Divine intervention? Southwark Cathedral is not St Pauls, of course (at the moment so much the better for that) and, unless he is to retrace his steps, given his route is directly past it what can he do other than go inside? Pausing on the threshold, he notices the name of the cathedral: St Saviour's.

As is always the case with houses of the Lord, Lawrence is struck by the cool of the building and the quality of the air inside. Massive stone walls soften and then bounce around the quiet chatter of the few people who have strayed inside, turning it into a reverent hum. Inevitably there are those progressing to or from the 'Golden Hind' and who have their phones to-hand, taking photographs of the pillars, the ceiling, the windows; but the majority seem to be doing nothing more than walking and looking. He stands, as he always does on such occasions, at the head of the central aisle and looks along the length of the church, west to east. There are six pillars either side of the nave before the openings to the short transepts; beyond that, the choir and the altar. Looking up, he marvels at the vaulted ceiling, the majesty of the engineering, and he is awestruck once again at the scale of belief which conceived - and then built - such a tribute. Walking clockwise, he strolls along the north aisle and past the north transept, past the vestry behind the choir, and then to the great expanse behind the altar. Along the way he pauses briefly to examine monuments and tombs - including a memorial to Shakespeare - before returning towards the entrance along the opposite side of the cathedral. Stopping near the choir-end of the nave, Lawrence notices four people sitting nearby, each respectfully distanced from the next as if they are inhabiting an invisible but private one-person bubble. Two are staring straight ahead, one is reading, and the other is motionless, head down. In some kind of reflex action he wants to check his watch yet refrains from doing so, partly because he is fully conscious of the time, but mainly because it feels sacrilegious to do so; time is almost an irrelevance in such a place. He fixes on a chair that seems to conform to the distance rules informally established by the quartet in front of him and makes his way to it, endeavouring not to trip or scrape another chair en route. Arriving at his destination, he sits.

From his new vantage point he scans the cathedral once again, along the north aisle, across the nave, up the the altar, and down the south aisle. This is less to reverify his location than ensure that he missed nothing of significance during his inspection. The gentle background thrum of voices remains, but he finds it comforting rather than intrusive. Satisfied he has established a kind of cocoon for himself, he looks toward the sixteenth century altar screen. When he finds himself trying to count the number of figures carved within it, he smiles; it is a juvenile diversion.

"So" he says to himself, silently, "here we are."

It is an invitation, the 'we' heavily loaded and aimed at a partner who may - or may not - choose to be present. He thinks of Tessa for a moment, wonders if she has ever been here, wonders what really happened with Penny, and then closes his eyes. After a few seconds any distinctive sounds he might have previously heard - a laugh, the click of a camera, or a specific phrase uttered by someone passing nearby - dissolve, and he becomes wrapped-up in a noise that is low frequency and persistent; it is a little like the purring of a fridge, but softer and on a lower register. He wants it to be a presence.

His eyes still closed, he tries to recall when he had first been aware of God, of the voice; attempts to reconstruct the sequence of events which had resulted in their coming together. If there had been initiative on his part, he cannot recall it. Had his desire to believe resulted in the voice - or was it the other way round? The two possibilities carry very different meanings, even if the outcomes would have been similar. Sequencing God's departure - the disappearance of the voice then leading to his loss of belief - Lawrence is inclined to believe the reverse was therefore true: he had chosen to believe and only then was he spoken too. Certainly when his mother was in her final days he had asked questions, offered God a deal: "do this for me and I will..." But he knows such trades are never accepted. Didn't his mother's death prove that? And what about now? Wasn't he - by sitting in St Saviour's, quietly, reverently, eyes closed - opening the door once again? There was no deal on the table, he simply wanted to believe again; he wanted a second chance at companionship and comfort, and, he supposed, a degree of certainty. These were difficult times and he needed help to get through them. Where else could he turn? He thinks of the memorial to Shakespeare sited within these very walls, and then the Globe theatre nearby; he thinks of the Folios, the plays, the Bard's words enshrined within both paperback and hardback covers and occupying a small portion of the shelves in his Lincoln library - and he resigns himself to the fact that, after all's said and done, they offer him nothing. He replays moments from his meeting with Dylan and Tessa, and it also strikes him that neither of them are able to provide him with what he needs - even if he struggles to find a name for it.

Opening his eyes, he sees a shaft of light spearing across the cathedral from one of the windows to his right. It settles on an expanse of chairs on the other side of the nave. A figure, newly sitting there, is bathed in the light and, were he of a more romantic persuasion, Lawrence could easily have attributed to the image a visitation or a blessing. And even though it is no such thing, he still wishes *he* were the one bathed in the light, and so looks up to its source and silently interrogates it, questions both unspoken and unformed. In a way it is another offering, another opportunity. Not sure what else he can do - nor what he should do - he returns his gaze to the screen then gradually allows his eyes to drop until they are focussed on the patch of cathedral floor visible between his slightly parted knees. It seems as good a spot as any.

Never mind the light, the windows, the monuments and tombs; if God's presence is everywhere then why should it not be in that currently private little spot visible to him only? Not having given up, and convinced he is doing something wrong, he closes his eyes once more and tells himself to concentrate - and then not to concentrate at all, but rather to empty his mind. Surely there is a trick, a way to prepare the ground, to plough the road.

Overwhelmed by the stresses of the day - the travel, his meeting, the walk along the river, too much thinking - Lawrence begins to feel himself slipping into the beginnings of slumber. His heart and breathing slowing, it is a peaceful place, and he is content to traverse to the edge of it as if he were approaching a deep and still pool. He plays with the image for a moment, imagines the soft ripples, the slight breeze off the water; he finds himself wanting to move further forward and allow the water to encroach around the soles of his shoes. And it is then that he hears it. A voice.

In his reverie, at first he thinks it is coming from the water; but then he drags himself away, eyes still closed, and back into reality. The voice is indistinct, unclear, but clearly of a different order to the general background thrum. Still head bowed, he opens his eyes half expecting to find there is something different about that small rectangle of floor between his feet. Yet even though nothing has changed, there is this new sound. He concentrates, and as he does so the voice becomes a little louder, a little more distinct. There are syllables, the building blocks of words; and then there are words themselves. And as he hears them, Lawrence realises that the voice is not within him as he had hoped, but behind him. He raises his head. Still the altar screen, and to his left and right people walk the aisles. The new sound has become an incantation, the words of the Lord's Prayer now unmistakeable. Slowly he looks round.

A man, just two rows behind him, is on his knees. There is devotion in his posture, cramped as he is between two rows of chairs. From what Lawrence can make out - thinning hair, smart jacket, proper shirt - there is nothing remarkable about this man. He is not - as far as Lawrence can tell - God. This is no visitation, no message; it is merely someone who has come into the cathedral to pray and who has chosen to sit too close to him. Lawrence looks forward again and up towards the ceiling. He smiles at himself. What had he expected after all? How could this random man provide, in any way, the answer to his questions? And what, in this intrusion, is there to reignite his belief? He had wanted to be close to God once more and all he has been rewarded with is interruption. He tries to resurrect the image of the pool but fails. Well, he tells himself, it was worth a try.

Standing, he scrapes the chair back a little; the sound causes one or two heads to turn. He looks to the praying man. There is no reaction. Checking his watch, he finds it is getting toward two o'clock; London Bridge station is just ten or fifteen minutes' walk away. He'll be back at King's Cross in plenty of time. Without any kind of pause, Lawrences abandons his punctured bubble (if, indeed, that's what it was) and heads directly for the exit at which point he turns toward Borough High Street without hesitation or backward glance.

~

"Tilt; what now Old Boy?"

As the road begins to turn to the left, I see William IV Street and know I could cut along it and down to the Strand. In a few minutes I could be at the Adelphi, demanding to see the manager. I could take on the role of the affronted playwright, the wronged artist; I could try and explain *Rust* to him, try and get him on-side, get Rhodri fired; I could demand, cajole, threaten. And beg? "Come on, Old Fruit; Tilt never begs."

But my heart wouldn't be in any of that, not right now. On another day perhaps, but not this one; not when I have been ganged-up on by both professional associates and history. In any event I am drawn to the entrance of the National Portrait Gallery which appears almost tangentially before me, its steps - like the Yellow Brick Road - suggesting a pathway to some kind of sanctuary. I have always liked the NPG; it is never too busy, always reverential. A place to commune perhaps - though with what? The ghosts of the past? I check my watch. I have time for a mooch, and then perhaps a coffee in the less exclusive café it now shares with the National Gallery. Maybe benevolence or wisdom will emanate from the captured faces of the wise: Wilde, Joyce, Shaw. And Noel Coward? Probably not. I think back to my Foyles visit. Perhaps I could find the ideal spot for the inevitable portrait that will be commissioned once *Rust* and what follows have confirmed my status. I pause at the first step, glance down to my jacket, catch a flash of the lining, admire my shoes, the ensemble of me, and then head in.

After spending just a few minutes in the temporary exhibition - a far too-modern take on portraiture which, to my eye, veers perilously close to graffiti - I head upstairs to the room containing portraits of the famous from the nineteenth- and twentieth-century. How long has it been since I was here last? I pause before a likeness of Churchill, almost as if he might have the answer to that question. Two years? Four? Yet there is still a familiarity about the place, like revisiting an old friend, one on whom you can rely - and there are far too few of those about these days. Friendship has become unfashionable. Like love, it has been replaced by the superficial and immediate, the swipe and the click, the chimera of reality television. "All ideas for the future, Tilt." Feeling the foundations of my next big idea beginning to gradually build, I determine not to let them crumble away and so head for a seat near the centre of the room from where I can scribble in my notebook, and gradually turn and absorb whatever these depictions of greatness have to transmit.

But what of these men? For they are nearly all men. How much do we know about them? In many cases their histories are as legendary as the images in front of me, images which have become popularised, trademarked like Shakespeare's signature. We know about Joyce's exile, his struggles with health, his obsessions, the difficulty of getting *Ulysses* published. And Wilde: *Reading Gaol, Dorian Grey* - and the conflicts with society brought about by his sexuality. And other, more obscure men? Those famous in their own fields and whose names may be known but not their lives? I scan beyond Wilde and Joyce and, from a distance, look into eyes of faces many of which I fail to recognise. And even when I do, I struggle to recall anything other than a name, an occupation, the legend of that one 'big thing' for which they are famous. When my portrait is hanging here - not in this room but elsewhere, perhaps on the bright balcony near the stairs - what will people see when they look into the reproduced eyes of The Great Tilt? Oh, some will know about *Rust* and how it was the turning point; they will know about the plays that followed, the triumphs. But what of the man? If they are a fan, they may know about Duncan or Julian, but not the nature of our meeting today; and they may know about Mimi and Amanda - something which is especially likely if, between now and then, Mimi sniffs an opportunity to get her name in lights, however low-wattage. But none of those people are me. In a way they hardly matter.

Will those future people standing in front of my portrait know for example, that - Mimi and Amanda notwithstanding - Tilt was no family man? Indeed, never was a family man; perpetually single in the legal sense, and which - gazing into the future as I do now - will have always remained the case. Theorists will ask whether such a status was maintained by choice or came about as a result of history, the inevitable outcome for an only child whose parents were both dead by the time he was twenty-five. "Nature," one might say; "Nurture," another. And maybe they'll look to the plays - post-*Rust* of course - for clues. Perhaps I should consider leaving them a trail, a tease of breadcrumbs. Some may wonder how I managed to maintain my independence given my effervescence, the circles in which I moved. They may even look at old photographs of Mimi or Amanda and shake their heads in baffled wonderment. "How was it possible he didn't marry?" How little they know. Certainly less than I do, the man on the inside, the gent with the scoop. Unless I one day confess all - on 'Arena', potentially - they'll never understand the nature of the double-edged sword that being extrovert brings with it. Or being a loaner, inevitable residue for an only child who grew up in a world increasingly inhabited by people he created and over whom he had complete control. Or both. I wonder whether some of these men who stare down from the walls would understand such tautology, such conflict. I'm sure some might.

And maybe other contemporaneous detectives will look upon my portrait and try and see the links between Tilt and his parents; or perhaps they may have done their research and come armed with knowledge of James and Willa Tillet. If so, theirs will be facts laced with prejudice and assumption. Indeed, hardly facts at all, because what could they really know? That each of Tilt's parents - in their own way and for their own particular reasons - just left him to get on with life, to work it out for himself, to build a universe in which he could be at the centre? Will they know about a father who was so introverted that he had trouble building a relationship with the face he saw in the mirror each morning when he shaved? Or a mother who became so absorbed in the local Am Dram society that it took over her every waking hour: planning, rehearsing, organising, performing? They may lazily assume that I have more to be grateful for to her than him: *The Discomforted* staged in memory of the remarkable Willa Tillet... Perhaps. But at least I know - and like - the face I see each morning in the bathroom mirror, the face of a public figure. "Dead by the time the Great Man was twenty-five," one of these detectives might echo about my father, loading their comment with pathos, "that's so sad." And they will ignore the fact that they had me later in life, that I missed growing up with youthful parents, and that even though I was young when - in their individual ways - they comprehensively left me, James was already over seventy, Willa getting on that way. I imagine a question, posed during an intimate televised interview, asking how I felt about coming late into their lives. "It made me what I am," I might say, somewhat cryptically. It is a universal answer. "And when they died?" the interviewer might press on. Ah, well...

Would I be practical or emotional at that point? What suggestions do these wall-hung faces surrounding me offer? In the main I see practical men: politicians, economists, medical or industrial pioneers. Men who stood for no nonsense, who revelled in right and wrong, black and white, no matter what might have been going on in their personal lives. We're all on that spectrum somewhere. Very well; the practical first. The twenty-five year old Tilt was suddenly very comfortable, financially-speaking. Insurance payouts, inherited pensions, a house worth far more than he had imagined. I was released to shape then live my dreams. Selling the old family home allowed me to move from my mangey flat into somewhere better: style, size, area. North London came into focus - and years later, being able to sell-up in Highgate funded my move to York, a place suddenly suitable for a citizen of my stature and reputation. Not being in town marked me out as being above mainstream tittle-tattle; Tilt didn't need it. So in York I embarked on the process of invention again, the process originally made possible by the dear departed actually departing. But what if that opportunity hadn't arisen just then, as it did? I glance at my shoes and notice a slight scuff on the toe cap of my left brogue; it is almost too small to be concerned about but, image being everything, nonetheless I lean forward and rub it lightly away with the palm of my left hand.

"And emotionally?" The interviewer might bring me back to the unanswered half of the question. I wonder what they will be expecting; what anyone who asked such a thing might want to hear. There are standard answers, aren't there? Words we reserve for such occasions, primed to slip from the tongue. And when we use them we're really avoiding the question, giving it no thought or true consideration. That might be an idea for a character in a play, someone who dodges reality, ducks and dives around it, toys with the others on the stage… I wonder if how I answer will depend on who's asking the question in the first place: male or female, young or old. There will be a rapport already established - or not. That will help me decide. "Devastated, heart-broken, cast adrift." If I'm not feeling up to the truth, then veneer would probably do. And if they asked me today - after meeting Duncan and Justin, the hiccup with *Rust*, the disquiet in Foyles, the intrusion of 'the historical women' - that certainly would be all they'd get. But if I've had a good day and the interviewer is female and young and pretty, if she's happy to let me flirt with her - even though I shouldn't, given the age gap ("Tilt, you rogue!") - then I might just play the honesty card. "How did I feel? Liberated, free, released. There would have been a moment of sadness I'm sure (though I don't recall how long it lasted), but their going allowed me to become the man I wanted to be." I have the recollection that from somewhere on these walls either Freud or Jung might be staring down on me. Freud, probably. He will have had a theory to which my answer either would or would not align; something about mothers and sons most likely. Or fathers and sons, but less so. And would my pretty interviewer leave it at that, or push on for more? "Tell me about *The Discomforted*," she might say, drawing a link between death and birth, the closing of one door and the opening of another. Perhaps she is wise beyond her years, this little minx who's asking the questions. "Be careful, Tilt; that one's a minefield!"

"Is it?"

I'm not so sure, voice. In what way?

I'd written the play a year or so before; had even discussed it with the old mater, floated the idea of her company taking it on. I said I was happy for her to direct it, that I trusted her. It was a gambit of course. I'm sure she mentioned it to someone because Ralph contacted me after her death, talked about a 'tribute'; but I'm not convinced she ever read it herself. I don't think she gave me any credit; she didn't believe I was capable of anything 'worthy'. Does that sound like I owed her such a debt? Mind you, the old pater didn't read it either, but at least his encouragement - if you can call it that - didn't rule anything out. "You can be what you want to be," he used to say, a vague generalisation used more often than not to get out of an uncomfortable conversation with his son. I heard it enough to begin to believe it. And then Ralph looked at the play, asked me to beef up one of the female characters and create a role that Willa herself would have loved to play. He called her Willa to my face, not 'your mother'. Five months later they put it on, Willa's name plastered all over the posters - and mine spelled incorrectly, like an afterthought no-one could be bothered to correct. Well, that's all different now, isn't it?

"Is it?"

Yes, it bloody well is. London, successes, a track record; and now, riding emblazoned over the horizon, *Rust* and everything that will presage. Of course it's different!

I wait for the voice - my voice - to contradict me but it remains silent. Looking around, Yates, Joyce, Churchill and the rest are all waiting for my next move, and with some discomfort I feel less allied to them. As if they are spying on me. Or that I'm the subject of a bizarre experiment. This absurd notion makes me realise how tired and in need of caffeine I am. Glancing at my watch, a little after one-thirty registers. Time enough then.

After the relative quiet of the NPG, the café is throbbing. Families and groups of tourists huddle around tables, carrier bags bearing the logo of the National Gallery very much in evidence. Although a bright, open and modern space, the background cacophony drags it down to some lower common denominator. I can't help but compare it to the British Library restaurant - both in terms of the establishment and its clientele - yet it is an unfair comparison which does this particular venue no favours; here they are catering for a different demographic, a mass market in just about every sense of the word. Standing in the centre of the large space for a moment, I try to establish a still point in the flow of people heading to and from the cloakrooms, to and from the counters and tables. I search for a strategy. It has been so long since I was down here, I feel vaguely shocked and disconcerted by the dynamism of the place. "Concentrate, Tilt!" I just need a strong coffee and perhaps something sugary to get me back to King's Cross in one piece. It is a simple requirement which - allied to the limited time available - rules out the refinement of Ochre, and forces me to settle on the Espresso Bar which seems a shade quieter than Muriel's Kitchen. As I wander over to join a surprisingly short queue, I can't help but wonder who Muriel is or was, and whether for those 'in the know' hers is a name which conjures excellence. Or is it a byword for something else? By the time I arrive at the Espresso Bar counter I have decided that the name is unlikely to have represented either a current or former member of the NG, having been chosen for its cosiness and nod to home cooking.

"Black Americano please - with an extra shot." I smile as I scan the counter, then point. "And one of those Danish pastries."

I flash a smile, but the young man serving me is too much a slave to his autopilot to do anything other than go through the motions. It is not that he's rude - far from it - but he's simply doing what's necessary to get him from A to B, the beginning of his shift to the end. A few moments later, armed with a small tray upon which my slightly over-expensive victuals rest, I turn and scan for somewhere to sit. As luck would have it, a small table-for-two is just being vacated in what appears to be a relatively quiet corner. Arriving there with the seats still warm, I shuffle the previous occupants' detritus to one side of the table and establish myself at the other. Nearby, a rack for used trays, crockery and cutlery awaits, and on the table in front of me - and here and there on the walls - polite notices asking patrons to clear their tables when they leave. Failure to follow such instruction is, I have found, a universally common fault. Were I in the mood I might be inclined to cut the guilty duo now walking towards the stairs a degree of slack; perhaps they do not speak or read English well, or perhaps wherever it is they come from café culture is quite different. And then the man says something to make his companion laugh and I hear the grating of a domestic accent. Well then.

It is a inditement which saddens me. Not the failure to comply as such, but rather the tangential notion that those two people now disappearing from view could one day be in my audience, potential punters, those for whom I sweat the proverbial blood and tears in order to offer them something to enrich their lives. And they can't even be bothered to clear a table! Doesn't striving to offer that enrichment drive what I do?

'Is it?'

If not, why do I do what I do then, voice? Isn't that what *Rust* and all the rest of it is about, to shed a light of some kind, to offer a modicum of wisdom or enlightenment? And - if you must - entertainment. And when I have written my next masterpiece, exposed some of the less often considered facets of love, the complexities and nuances of attachment, will it be wasted on people like those two now out of sight? But then surely they would never go to one of my shows... I catch myself feeling ungenerous again. They have come to the National Gallery after all; doesn't that say something? Anything? It is a simple question which, at this moment, seems too difficult to answer, and so I turn my attention to the pastry sitting on the plate in front of me, waiting to be demolished. Did they have such pastries on the menu at the BL? It would have been a statement alternative to Duncan and Justin's lemon drizzle. But if I *had* indulged, having an unfinished morsel on my plate might have made my exit slightly more problematic. Again those two return to me, and so I try to ease them away by concentrating on my Danish, breaking it into suitably sized chunks with the fork the lad behind the counter gave me. Fork rather than knife; was that appropriate?

Between first and second mouthfuls I am suddenly conscious of a shadow over my table. Assuming it to be a member of staff clearing, I look up and am surprised to find myself faced with a woman wearing a roll-neck wool jumper, coat slung over one arm. She smiles a little nervously.

"I'm sorry to interrupt," she begins, the slight faltering in her voice supporting the statement she has just made, "and I expect you get this all the time..." A second hesitation, as if she is weighing up whether or not to carry on. "But aren't you that famous writer, Mr. Tilt?"

Having estimated her to be in her mid- to late-thirties, the fact that she has recognised me - and called me 'famous'! - permits me to take five years off her. Perhaps she has only recently turned thirty. I offer her the best professional smile I can muster. Given everything that has been going through my head in the last hour or so, living up to the billing she has given me suddenly feels a little more difficult than it ought.

"Yes, I am. Thank you." Although she has done nothing which requires thanks - other than recognise me - I have always found doing so sets people at ease. And her recognition of me justifies just a little acknowledgement.

On past occasions when I have been accosted in such a manner, at this point two things usually happen: either the person concerned asks for an autograph, or they simply walk away satisfied to have made the briefest of connections. Expecting one or the other, I am surprised when the woman does neither.

"I just wanted to say," the hesitation is still there, but she has calmed down a little, "how much I admire your work." She laughs, as if she is aware how trite and clichéd the statement sounds. It is of course, but how can we tire of ever hearing it? "And particularly your new play, *The Colour of Rust*."

"*Rust*?" I find myself hoping the surprise in my voice isn't too evident.

"If you have a moment… I know I'm interrupting."

I motion to the chair opposite, but rather than immediately take it, the woman lifts the offending tray belonging to the table's previous occupants and conveys it to the trolley where she slides it in half-way down. I confess to being slightly mesmerised by the novelty of the encounter. When she returns to the table, she stands opposite me again forcing me to repeat the invitation to sit. I feel grateful that she has given me a second opportunity to dismiss her.

"Charlotte Lockwood," she says on sitting, offering me her hand. I take it, briefly.

"So you liked *Rust*?" Glancing down to my part-finished pastry and coffee, I cut to the chase.

"Yes, very much." She follows my gaze. "You're sure it's okay; I mean if you have a minute."

"Yes, of course - though I have to be away fairly soon." I prepare the ground for my escape, just in case she turns out to be an unsavoury character.

As she weighs up her next move I evaluate her further. The jumper looks good quality, as does the coat; and although she is wearing jeans, at least they are Levi's. Her make-up is subtly applied (what little of it there is) and she wears two rings on her right hand - both look gold - and none on her left. A professional person, and probably a successful one at that.

"I thought it was quite remarkable," she begins, trying to sound relaxed but with urgency in her voice as if she knows she is under time-pressure and might be dismissed at any moment.

"How so?"

"Because it was so different from your previous work - which I also loved, by the way."

"You're very kind."

"But it seemed to me that with *The Colour of Rust* you were moving on, heading somewhere else. Watching it, I felt as if I was witnessing something new. There was something in that character, Charles, I hadn't seen before in your plays: edgy, complex, nuanced. And in a way, remarkably honest. Even dangerously so."

I feel my day taking a turn for the better.

"That's very generous of you. And very perceptive. I was particularly pleased with him." I find myself unable to leave it there, praise for the play having been so thin on the ground. "It's a shame there aren't more people who think like that."

"You mean the reviewers?"

I nod. She carries on.

"I read some of the reviews before I went. Obviously I didn't know what I was going to find... Some of them made me wonder whether I might be wasting my time; but having seen your other work - all the way from *The Discomforted* - how I could I not go?"

"Then I am grateful you persevered and chose to be one of the few who did, Charlotte. When did you see it?"

She pauses as she tries to locate her visit to the Adelphi in some kind of mental calendar.

"Not too long after it opened."

"And luckily before it's going to close." As soon as I have spoken I am annoyed; it feels as if I have let my guard down.

Why should I be sharing such information with a complete stranger? If my face clouds, Charlotte appears not to notice.

"But that's dreadful!" She seems genuinely affronted on my behalf. "It's such a brave piece."

"Brave?" My heart skips a little at the word; it is exactly what I would have wanted someone to say to me.

"Because it's a departure. Because it's new. Oh, I don't know that much about the theatre obviously, but that's how it seemed to me."

There is a short pause. I need hear nothing else from her now that she has uttered the word 'brave'. I want to explicitly thank her for rescuing my day, but to do so would be to knowingly cross a line. Or to risk taking advantage of someone who has just wanted to share their thoughts with me.

She mistakes my not responding for something else.

"But I've said too much; taken up too much of your time."

There is a sudden flatness in her tone, and I find myself not wanting her to leave with any misunderstanding. She needs to realise I have appreciated the trouble she has taken. It is, perhaps, a little out of character for me - but then it has been an unusual day thus far.

"What do you do, Charlotte?" I spear a chunk of pastry in such a way as to suggest that I actually want to hear her response and am prepared to wait for it; to generate the notion - however fleeting - that we're just a couple of old pals having coffee together.

"Me?"

I nod and place the cake in my mouth.

"I'm a buyer. I mean, I work in fashion. For M&S. Part of a team that looks for and then secures new products." She pauses, unsure if she should go on, or if she has already gone too far. "I get to travel sometimes; you know, overseas. It's a busy life."

"Then I'm even more appreciative of you taking time out to watch one of my plays." Her body language tells me that the flattery has clearly worked. "And I'm not surprised."

"That I went to see one of your plays?"

I smile, realising I have confused her.

"No. Your job. There's something elegant about your jumper; it immediately suggested to me a woman who knew something about clothes and what does - and does not - look good."

It's an honest statement - and under the circumstances one might even say 'brave'. Reminiscent of a younger Tilt. I try to convey the wisdom of the older version of myself, to get my smile to suggest that I mean nothing by my comment other than to compliment her. Years ago what I have just said might have passed for an undisguised chat-up line, the bait on a hook. Did Mimi or Amanda fall foul of such a gambit? I cannot recall. In any event, Charlotte's blushing suggests I have done nothing but confuse her.

"That's kind of you," she says, the hesitancy having returned. She pauses for just a moment then rises, repeating herself as she does so. "I've already taken too much of your time. And I expect your coffee will be getting cold because of me."

I make a dismissive motion as if to sweep her objection aside. But she is settled on her next course of action. She offers me her hand for the second time.

"It's been wonderful to meet you. Thank you. I just wanted you to know… You know."

"It's been lovely to meet you too, Charlotte." The practiced professional smile. "And I really do appreciate your taking the trouble. You have no idea how valuable feedback such as yours can be."

She smiles and glances down at the table, then back up to me. With a nod - more of relief than anything else I suspect - she offers a brief "Bye" then turns and walks toward the cloakrooms. Picking up my coffee and taking a sip (and it *has* gone a little cold) I watch her as she heads away, part of me expecting a pause, a glance over the shoulder, even a little wave. But she does none of those things and, for a reason I can't fathom, I find I'm more glad than not.

Finishing my pastry I check my watch again. The morning having dragged its feet thus far, this time I'm surprised to find it's getting on for two o'clock. Taxi back to King's Cross then. I stand, place my empty cup and plate back onto the tray and then glance over to the counter where, having just been served, a couple are scanning the café looking for a free table. My movement has attracted their attention, and though trying to look nonchalant, they are evidently poised to pounce. I nod toward them, giving them permission to approach, then lift my own tray and head for the rack. When I pass the table again on my way out they have already arrived.

"Thank you," the man says.

"You're welcome," is my inevitable reply. It feels a little like a small victory, though over what I am unable to say.

Walking towards the exit I glance to the toilets half expecting to see Charlotte emerge, for coincidence to take a hand. But she does not, and - uncertain whether or not I'm disappointed - I abandon the café for the bustle of Charing Cross Road once again.

14:00

Toby's phone vibrates in his pocket, its doing so surprising him - and then he recalls how he had switched it to silent as he waited to go into Tyrell's consulting room. Retrieving it from his pocket, he slides the toggle to restore sound and then checks the screen. Marita. He had forgotten they had agreed she would call him at two.

"Hi," he says.

"Where are you?" Her clipped tones are exaggerated by the phone, her distance from him, as if all the softness had been filtered out somewhere between here and Peterborough. "It sounds like you're in a washing machine or at a racetrack."

Uncertain how she could possibly know what being inside a washing machine sounds like, Toby stops walking and looks at the myriad of vehicles on Euston Road. One might choose to view it as a racetrack.

"Euston Road," he answers. "It's all the traffic. Sorry if it's noisy but I'm walking back to the station."

"Walking?"

He wonders why she should be surprised. Perhaps there had been an outcome to his visit he hadn't previously considered - and a calamitous one at that. Yet it wasn't in Marita's nature to be overtly pessimistic.

"Of course. Why shouldn't I be?"

"I don't know. It seems such a big step forward from how you've been."

"I don't think it was actually as bad as I made out. I mean, in using the crutches I was just trying to be a good boy." Toby waits a moment to see if his joke garners any kind of response. "In fact I've been walking around Regent's Park."

"On your crutches?" Marita slips seamlessly into her default mode of wanting facts, details.

"Only one."

"So what did he say?"

"Tyrell? That I was making decent progress and didn't need both crutches; that one would do. In fact he sort of said that I could stop using that one as soon as I was able. Which is one of the reasons for the walking, to try out my heel and see how it feels with a bit more strain on it."

"So how does it feel?"

Toby flexes his Achilles by rotating his ankle slightly, then leans against it and his stick in concert. Without doubt it feels less comfortable than it had an hour previously. He looks up and along Euston Road trying to gauge the distance remaining to King's Cross. It's further than he thought, but he has time enough.

"Pretty good. I can tell it's working harder, of course; it's throbbing a little, but that's just a sign that it's getting better."

"Really?" Marita sounds unconvinced.

Looking along the road in the opposite direction, Toby watches two vacant cabs rush from the west towards and then past him. His fallback option.

"How are the kids? Did they get off to school okay?" He changes the subject.

"Yes, fine - though Lucy was coughing a little bit over breakfast. I think there's something going round the school."

"Isn't there always?"

"I'll see how she is later. We've got some of those chewy children's paracetamol I can give her if I need to."

It is a statement whose banality flummoxes him. If there are a range of potential responses available to him in order to keep up his end of the exchange he has forgotten them all. He imagines himself facing a serve in tennis and suddenly finding he has no racket. Or worse, a full-length yorker with his hands empty, his bat having been left behind in the pavilion. How did that happen?

"When do you think you'll be back?" Marita's question punctures the image. Obscurely, Toby imagines hearing his stumps shatter.

"Train's at three, which means I should be in Peterborough just before four. So about half-past four, if the train's on time."

"And what do you want for tea? I thought sausages and that cauliflower cheese left over from the other night."

Toby wonders why, if Marita had the answer to her question already, she bothered to ask him. Ignoring the mundanity of it, he has a sudden desire for her to be suggesting something more exotic, as if being down to a single crutch is something to be celebrated. Sausages and cauliflower fail to fit the bill on so many levels.

"Sounds fine." he pauses just a moment. "I'd better crack on and finish my walk. Don't want to miss the train."

"Oh," she calls him back before he signs off, "Huw rang here a while ago. He'd forgotten you were in London today."

"Huw?"

"Said could you give him a call at some point."

"Okay, will do."

And then they are separated again, the closing of the call reinstating the seventy or so miles between them. Toby wonders if that's what phones did, collapse distance, make it malleable. Time travel, in a way. Surely the stuff of science fiction.

Beginning his slow march eastwards, once he is back into an acceptable rhythm he flicks to the contacts list on his phone and scrolls down until he finds Huw's name, pressing the 'call' button without thinking.

"Hello?"

When Sandi's voice surprises him, Toby realises he had selected their home number rather than Huw's mobile.

"Hi, Sandi, it's Toby. Is Huw there?" Bluffing time.

"Toby." She pauses for a fraction of a second. "He's still at work I'm afraid."

"Of course." Toby feigns stupidity. "He rang me and for some reason I thought he was at home."

"Try his mobile. Where are you? It sounds awfully noisy."

"London. And it is." He is amazed how detached she sounds, considering.

"Doing anything exciting?"

If he waits for a moment before replying he does so telling himself it isn't because he's hoping she is going to follow her question with a suggestion: "what are you doing tomorrow afternoon?"

"Exciting? Unfortunately not. Not today." Another moment, another space which could be filled. "I'll give him a shout on his mobile then. Sorry to have disturbed you."

As he goes back to his contacts' list, Toby tries to reconcile the brief exchanges with Sandi and Marita. Two voices in close juxtaposition, varnish applied to different parts of his life, to different experiences. For a moment he imagines their accents blended together to create some kind of contemporary but stateless Englishness; echoes of Hollywood's mid-century mid-Atlantic twang perhaps. But it is an exercise relating to more than just how they sound. If anything, it centres on what those voices have come to represent: routine versus liberation, perhaps; drudgery against adventure; the mechanical facing off against the passionate.

A call to Huw will hardly help distil one from the other. Overlaying aural evidence of his cricketing life simply adds to the mix, a symphonic trio playing the occasionally discordant theme tune of his existence.

"There you are," Huw says. "Glad you got my message. Sorry, I forgot you were in London - that is if I knew in the first place."

"No problem. What's up?"

"Nothing major. Just wanted to remind you about the committee meeting tomorrow and check that you were still available."

"Of course."

"Usual agenda: fees and fixtures; talking about the juniors. You know."

And Toby did indeed know. They had been following the same pattern for as long as he could remember; an evening of bonhomie and promise, looking forward to a future season that surely would be their best ever. This time, this time…

But if it was so predictable did that make it routine too, his first love turned to mechanical drudgery? How can that be true given cricket elevates his life from such a quagmire. Toby feels a frisson of excitement - then a throb of reminder from his Achilles.

"What did he say?" Huw asks.

"Who?"

"The Doc."

"Good news. Almost a clean bill of health. I should be off the crutches really soon." Toby wonders if he could manage going to tomorrow's meeting without his one remaining support. It is only a small step to his next white lie. "Should be in light training and ready for the first nets in March."

Another stab from his ankle. On Euston Road a cab toots at someone making a late manoeuvre.

~

Imogen's phone rings just as she is crossing the concourse of London Bridge Station, heading for the underground.

"Hi Vic," Imogen says a little too loudly, just as the station announcer blasts news of a delay to the assembled throng.

"Where are you?!" Victoria is clearly taken aback.

"London Bridge; heading for the underground. Can you hear me okay?"

"So? How was it?"

Although slightly difficult to pick-up, Imogen can't help but notice the upbeat tone in Victoria's voice. It resonates with both fear and hope, the former for herself, the latter in wishing that her friend had done well. Imogen - torn between the truth and not wanting to disappoint - weighs up her options. Being honest, right here, right now, is not palatable; in part because she wants to break the news face-to-face in order to better control the message, but also because she is reasonably certain that she has yet to adequately process the day herself.

"Good, actually." Imogen pauses for a moment, deciding to ease herself in via the concrete. "And the building! So tall! Highest in Europe I think."

"How far up were you?"

"Oh, probably half-way. And the views were wonderful! Right across London. I think you need to be really high up to realise just how vast it is. You know, like when you're flying into Heathrow. Probably. And the office was luxurious compared to ours: machines that gave out proper coffee - and hot chocolate. Bottles of fizzy water. And those little wrapped-up mints, you know?"

"And the people?"

From Victoria's tone, Imogen can tell her little narrative is going down well.

"Very nice. In fact the HR guy - Anthony - was rather dishy. I bet he has all the girls after him!"

"And will you add your name to that list?" Victoria laughs.

"Very funny, Vic." Imogen allows a long enough pause to introduce a change of tone. "I'm not sure to be honest. I mean, they haven't said anything yet - said it would be next week in any case - but there's a lot to weigh up."

"But the building, Anthony, London!" Victoria sounds slightly incredulous.

"I know; but it's about more than that isn't it? I mean, the job's got to be right, hasn't it? And I met the man who'd be my boss."

"Not so nice?"

"No, no; nice enough. But let's just say I didn't warm to him as much. Maybe he was having a bad day."

"But from what you've said to me before even Jack the Ripper would be better than Sonia!"

Although she can't remember the comment, it is enough to make Imogen laugh - just as another blast on the tannoy announces an imminent departure. She takes it as a cue.

"Look, I've got to go Vic; tube back to King's Cross and all that. If I don't see you tomorrow we'll catch-up at the weekend, okay?"

"Okay. I'll call you."

Imogen looks at her silenced phone before she slips it back into her bag. What happens to those words after they have flown to Stevenage and been absorbed by Victoria? With a smile she imagines an enormous landfill site where all the words used in telephone conversations - and which are no longer needed - are piled up awaiting disposal. How do you dispose of words? And if so, is there a second site where all the little white lies are segregated? If it was possible to re-use phrases from either dump, which ones would be picked up first?

At the top of the escalator, she stares down into the bowels of the station, momentarily mesmerised by the bright chrome, the colourful posters, the stark lighting. These are the entrances to the dark tunnels that will take her from here and deposit her elsewhere, a journey unseen by anyone on the surface - and without remark from her fellow travellers. She wonders how many of those professional-type women she will see at this time of day.

A man bumps her left shoulder as he hurries past, walking down the escalator to get to his own destination just a little bit faster, perhaps making an earlier train. She shifts her bag a little on her shoulder and knows this will be her last trip on the underground for some time.

~

Lawrence's phone rings when he is half-way along St. Thomas' Street. Across the road from him an ambulance emerges from the nearby hospital and offers a brief blast of its siren before turning toward Borough High Street. He glances at his phone's screen: 'number withheld'.

"Hello?"

"What was that? Where are you?"

Recognising Tessa's voice, he laughs.

"Heading for the station; near Guy's, hence the ambulance."

A slight hiatus is sufficient for him to stop walking.

"Can you hear me, Tessa?"

"I just wondered how you were."

"I'm fine. Really."

Another pause.

"And our meeting?"

Lawrence wonders in what context Tessa intended him to respond to her open-ended question: their meeting in what sense?

"As I expected, I suppose." He plays it safe. "I mean, it was good to see you."

"You too."

Again there is something unsaid in his sister's statement.

"Dylan was - what?" Lawrence shifts the conversation away from them. It seems safer ground, temporarily at least.

"Just Dylan." She laughs, more to herself than him. "He was exactly as I expected him to be."

"Still angry?"

"Permanently so, I think. And not just at you. Sometimes I think he feels as if life has a grudge against him."

"But today was my turn to be in the firing line."

In the short pause that follows, Lawrence imagines Tessa scanning wherever she is for clues as to her next move.

"He was hurt deeply, you have to recognise that. Yes, he's full of attitude and bluster, and in a way the bully he always was - but that doesn't mean he wasn't upset."

Expecting confirmation, he is at first surprised by Tessa's response - but then quickly reconciles it as being an example of how his sister is; how considerate and conciliatory she has always been. Lawrence wonders whether there is any merit in dissecting Dylan's character any further - and decides it would be pointless.

"And you?" He brings it back to the two of them.

"Me? In what sense?"

"Were you upset?"

"By you?" Tessa doesn't wait for a response. "I was upset in all sorts of ways. I was angry at Mum for dying and Dad for not being there, at Dylan for - well, being Dylan. And you? Yes, of course. How could I not be?"

There is something cathartic for Lawrence in hearing her admission as if by naming him it is cleansing, confirming. Perhaps it is also something Tessa has held on to for far too long; if so, surely it might be good for her as well.

"And I was angry at Penny too." She surprises him again.

"Penny?"

"I think we were winding down even then - if that's a phrase I can use. I expected her - no needed her - to be more supportive back then, but I think she'd already stopped caring quite as much as she had before."

It was, Lawrence imagines, an abandonment which may have been as significant for Tessa as God's had been for him. He reconstructs the image he has of Tessa as she returned to their café table from the lavatory. Accurate or not, he labels it betrayal personified.

"That must have been hard." He waits for her to step into the gap he leaves. The phone is silent. "Sis?"

"Sorry." She is back with him. "I was just distracted by something. You were saying?"

"You should come to Lincoln." He changes tack. "For a weekend. Get away from the city."

Taking his statement as a cue he begins walking again, and even though it has always been there in the background, he feels the noise of the street intrude again on the call. He imagines the sound forcing Tessa to reconstruct her own tapestry of the city she presumably knows too well. Hers will be a more complete and more detailed sketch than his own. And more tolerant? He thinks of the crowds of tourists, the fake reconstructions of history, the remorseless and uncaring river.

"That would be nice. Let me check my diary when I get home and maybe I'll email you…"

He wonders where she is if she is not at home; there is no backing track of traffic to give him a clue. And then her word 'maybe' hovers before him.

"That would be good. We could go to the cathedral and have a proper chat, without distractions or intrusions."

By intrusions is he referencing London or Dylan? Or Penny or God? Or all of them, the quartet which - one way or another - may have betrayed both of them. Closing the call, he knows Tessa will be drawing her own lines between the dots he has laid out.

~

"Tilt" says a voice. Duncan.

Ringing as it does while the cab waits at Cambridge Circus, the junction with Shaftesbury Avenue, the phone call breaks me from my reverie, one of those odd moments when one is between here and there staring vacantly and not really looking. If I have been clinging to echoes of Charlotte's affirming words, hearing Duncan's voice bursts that particular bubble like a pin through rubber.

"Duncan."

"On your way home?"

"Stuck - as ever - on Charing Cross Road; which is, as I'm sure you know, merely the apéritif for the delights of Tottenham Court Road."

"Indeed." A pause. "I wondered if you might have gone to the Adelphi."

"The Adelphi?" I try and make the idea sound foolish, as if the Great Tilt would even entertain such a notion. "Why would I want to go there?"

"I don't know. To try and talk some sense into Webster."

"Is that his name?"

"Yes." Another small pause. "Maybe I thought you might try and persuade him not to close. Or try and get Rodri fired."

"The very thought." I throw in a short laugh which is coincident with the cab moving again. "Haven't we drawn a line under the Adelphi? You made it perfectly clear that there was no going back, no option to be pursued. It was delivered as a fait accompli."

"You were upset."

Duncan's shallow perspicacity stuns me. A phrase I have heard elsewhere - 'no shit, Sherlock' - pops into my head and I smile. Refraining from comment for a moment, just as the cab pauses again - this time outside Foyles - I am propelled back in time to stand amidst their shelves, the drama section, the space awaiting my book. And so I find myself having to deal with Justin again too.

"Indeed."

"And I can understand that, but…"

"But?"

"To just walk out… Hardly constructive."

He must be feeling either combative or put out to even hint at criticism, however mild. Perhaps I had embarrassed him; perhaps Justin passed comment. If I had made Duncan uncomfortable, then mission accomplished.

"As you say, Duncan, I was upset. Call it 'artistic temperament' if you want to; I believe that excuses a multitude of sins in our game."

Did he appreciate my offer to include him on the same side as me, the suggestion that we were somehow 'in it together'? Without being able to see whether he felt puffed up or put out, I have nothing really to go on. Which is one of the beauties of the stage of course, being able to say so much without a character speaking a single word. It is, I think, one of my greatest areas of strength. If I had thought to ask Charlotte I'm sure she would have concurred. For a fleeting second I wish she was sitting alongside me so that I could do so now.

"Well, I just wanted to make sure you were - okay."

"How could I not be 'okay'?"

"I don't know. You might have decided to do something rash."

"Like go the Adelphi and kick the shit out of Webster?" Of course I had remembered his name all along.

"Something like that."

And then it strikes me that Duncan is not in the least worried about me, but rather about himself. The notion that the Great Tilt might have gone off in a huff to tear up his contract, to seek another, more competent Duncan - that would have perturbed him most of all. Perhaps both Duncan and Justin were unsettled in such a way. Did they talk themselves into the fear that I would be calling them next week to announce I had found a new agent, a different publisher? Surely if I wanted I could have a queue forming at my splendid oak front door. A trip to York? Not a problem to secure the signature of the Great Man. It is an idea which accompanies me as the cab crosses Oxford Street.

Yet is ditching Duncan a notion I actively toyed with in the aftermath of my exit stage left? I mean, really and seriously considered? Never mind the theatrics. And if I had not, should I have? Should I do so now, to while away the time on Tottenham Court Road, or on Euston Road, or on the three o'clock train north? Instinct tells me it is too soon, too close to making Duncan's fear - of doing 'something rash' - a reality. Perhaps it is better considered after a good meal, sitting in my study under the joint influence of my splendid bookcase and a couple of glasses of decent Chablis.

Again I am roused by Duncan's voice as he seeks to confirm we are still connected. "By a thread" I find myself thinking.

"Yes, still here. And no, Duncan, nothing rash - unless you count a quick visit to the National Portrait Gallery out of order. And where - you might be interested to know - I was accosted by a fan who said she thought *Rust* was brilliant, the best thing I have ever done."

The hook baited, I wait for a response. Duncan says nothing immediately. Perhaps he knows there is nothing he can say. And then he surprises me.

"Then we should get her to go and run the Adelphi."

It is a joke which takes me aback such that I can't help but laugh out loud. I catch the cabbie glancing in his mirror. Raising an eyebrow, I incline my head toward the phone to confirm the source of my sudden jollity. He goes back to driving.

"Perhaps we should. I have her name and where she works if you'd like to follow up on that."

Duncan duly laughs at my riposte.

"Well then," he says, and I can't help but catch a note of relief in his voice. "Look, give me a call in a week or so - once the dust has settled - and we can talk about what comes next."

Which does does he have in mind? The dust on the undisturbed seats at the theatre? The dust on my collected plays manuscript as it sits waiting on Justin and Kaley's desks? Or the dust gathering on my contract with Duncan? Perhaps he feels that particular coating has been disturbed - my sudden leaving the BL would have swirled particles in the air - and he wishes it to come to rest again, as if a fine layer sitting over the top of it acts as some kind of protection for him. Or a sign that all is well.

"Next?" I think about the ideas I've already had. Love, in all its guises. Including the pecuniary and base ones. My little Charing Cross Road prostitute - or perhaps Mimi. "Good idea," I say, offering an olive branch. Through the window I see the entrance to what used to be Heal's; doorways to 'colleges' which fleece foreign students endowed with more money than sense; a shiny Paperchase. In a way different versions of luxury. And luxury in love? "I'll call you. Probably next week. Or the week after." Dismissed.

I check my watch. Plenty of time to make the train.

15:00

As the train begins to draw out of the station, the guard's voice intrudes again to reconfirm their stopping points.

"This is the fifteen-hundred service to York, calling at: Stevenage, Peterborough, Grantham, Newark Northgate, Retford, Doncaster and York."

If you had missed the destination list the first time round, it would now be too late to recognise you had boarded the wrong train: you were now going at least as far as Stevenage whether you wanted to or not.

In the three-quarter-full first class compartment at the front of the train a flurry of replicated activity ensues: people checking watches or mobile phones, opening laptops or books, rustling in bags for snacks or drinks. One or two close their eyes more in hope than expectation, wanting sleep to speed them on their way. Only those travelling to York can enjoy the security of knowing they cannot possible doze beyond their destination and can therefore truly give themselves up to rest. But if you are going to Stevenage or Peterborough, either as a final destination or to change trains to get to Lincoln perhaps, then attempting sleep is to court disaster and waking up to find yourself further north than you had wanted to travel.

Notes

During the period in which this story is set the National Portrait Gallery was in fact closed, undergoing significant building work prior to its reopening in the summer of 2023.